AF480310

THIS HOLE WAS MADE FOR (YOU AND) ME

SIENNA EGGLER

BENEKEID INK, LLC

Copyright © 2023 by Sienna Eggler

All rights reserved.

No part of this book may be used for the training of or use by artificial intelligence, nor reproduced, distributed, or transmitted in any form or by any means, including photocopying, recording, or other electronic or mechanical methods, without the prior written permission of the publisher, except as permitted by U.S. copyright law.

The story, all names, characters, and incidents portrayed in this production are fictitious. No identification with actual persons (living or deceased), places, buildings, and products is intended or should be inferred.

Map of Lexanard by hiisikoloART

For content notes, see: https://www.siennaeggler.com/content-notes/

ALSO BY EGGLER

Early Adopter

Fluid Bonding

In the Company of Wolves

Never Too Much

The Threads That Weave

Last Train Home

Off the Beaten Path

This Hole Was Made For (You And) Me

St. Acton

Prequel: Gone Was the Glow

I Think of You Often

Learn more at www.siennaeggler.com/books/

BAYETTEK
DOYEMERE
LEXANARD
Ashfort
SILVERSTONE MINE
REDADORE
Saincaster
FLOWER FIELDS
Zachick
LAEFORD
Candle Cove
CLARK MEADOWS
RAGING RIVER
CALDERA SEA
N
E
S
W

CONTENTS

1

A BITTER AFTERTASTE

Meike rubbed their arm, mindful of the bandage and the wound beneath. They passed the bundle of colorful cloth to the pale-haired woman, averting their gaze from the ruined fabric. "I'm sorry…"

"For what?" Anniken held the poncho in a way that obscured her expression, and her tone was neutral. Annoyed, maybe? Or just tired?

"I ruined the equipment you made me."

"Silly Meike," she said, sighing. "Here, I'll get this patched up by the end of the week. But what happened?"

Where to even start? "There was a misunderstanding…I failed a summoning ritual and suffered the consequences."

"That…" She lowered the poncho to meet their eyes. "Was it that wolf?"

That look added years to Meike's life, but they mustered a soft affirmation. "I'm going to try again soon. It would've been fine, had I not stumbled over my words."

"If you're sure." She folded the poncho and draped it over her arm. "What are you going to do in the meantime?"

"Make those potions for you—and some extra healing pots for the rest of the party." That was the original plan, anyway. At any rate, it gave them something to do, and more time to catch up with Moira.

"Get on with it, then. I will warn you that Cass has something planned. A small party, from the sounds of it."

"A party..." As long as there was a vegetarian dish for them! Good food and company would do them well.

They met up with Moira later that morning, in a flower shop a short distance from her apartment. She carried a basket in one arm, filled with an assortment of herbs and mysterious plants from the market.

"Do you normally buy flowers," they said, feeling slightly out of bounds. Meike only recognized a few of these, and they were definitely not for consumption.

"You've only been to my home a few times," she said, laughing. "I normally buy and grow my own plants, but my last batch were...displaced during spring."

Meike gently ran a finger along the frond of a tall plant. "Did someone take them?"

"A neighbor. He's a real jerk and complained about it lowering the property value." She snorted and rolled her eyes. "I found them all scattered on the cobblestones below."

"That's awful..."

"Ah, but that's life, isn't it? It's a nice area, and it's near the market, but I may move before winter." She handed the clerk a handful of coins and led them outside.

There was no doubt in Meike's mind that she would stay in Laeford; her whole life was here. Question was, where would she go? The inn was all Meike knew, and so far no other domicile called their name. But a small shop, like Griselda's, and a personal garden was their ideal setup.

"I hope you find what you're looking for."

"Don't worry about me," she said. "I already have a few places in mind, and one even has a small balcony. It's further than I care for, but also closer to the sea..." She briefly closed her eyes, a soft smile creeping across her face. "Who knows, maybe I'll have it next time I see you? Oh Meike, it's going to be simply divine! I'll have an extra room to perform my crafts, so I'm not renting space or roughing it in my kitchen."

"I'm jealous already! I'd love a place of my own, but I'm not ready to settle down." Laeford was grand, but like Pickles said, there was more to explore beyond that.

"Please consider sticking around. I'd miss you."

"Aw, you'll be fine! You have Effie." And Meike had...who, exactly? Ignoring their current status, Anniken had Laken, Pickles his many lady friends, and Cass didn't seem interested in anyone. Well, she had Jasper.

And Meike had their furry little friends, but lacked the common language to bond over shared interests or discuss obscure topics.

"How's your arm, by the way?"

"Better!" The wounds healed fast, thanks to her handiwork, and even the marks were fading. Most were superficial wounds, but the few that weren't showed signs of scarring.

"Good, good. Have you played around with the counter yet?"

Right, her old AC...

After leaving Moira that day, they returned to their small room and curled up in bed. Alone and without the company of their familiars, they cried themself to sleep and woke up starving. It was past midnight, and unable to seek food from the kitchen or vendors, they snacked on the few food items at hand: hard, bitter apples, dried mushrooms, and a bread roll.

And once the food ran out, Meike turned to their new toy—the AC.

Studying that was how they spent the next few hours. It came without a manual and Moira gave little instruction, but they preferred this. The AC was a lovely puzzle and piece of tech, and by morning Meike knew the ins and outs, and even tapped into the local quest board. Their only complaint was the size and lack of a touchscreen. It was tiny and sat in the palm of their hand, like one of those virtual pets from their youth—such as a Tamagotchi or Digivice.

The PDA was dark blue with three red buttons, faded from time and use. One acted as a home button, another allowed them to scroll through their feed, and the third was the "select" button. As expected, the virtual keyboard was vastly inefficient and a real pain to slog through.

But their very own AC! Unfortunate for Moira, in that they'd have to rely on snail mail unless she bought a new counter, or upgraded to a PDA.

"It's nice, but I wish it had a keychain."

"My fault." She rubbed the underside of her jaw. "I wore it as a necklace, but you can attach a small chain to wear on your belt, if you'd like. Even a simple string would do!"

"I'll ask for a cord." They could show it off to Anniken at the same time. She'd get a kick out of this!

They stepped into Moira's apartment, and a wave of familiarity rushed over them. It had only been a day since the last visit, but Meike still basked in this moment, knowing it would be awhile before they returned.

"Vivica's doing well, by the way. She's settled down remarkably fast, but animals have to be adaptable. They never know what the day will bring."

"That was my assumption. I think she'll be ready to try again soon. I'll just have to make up for it with more walks and some meat!" It pained them to do so, but maybe a rabbit or two would appease the slighted wolf. They'd catch and prepare some just for her, maybe even make a thin broth with some of the choice bits.

"Let's focus on that later." She carefully set her bag on the kitchen counter and worked her through it, talking all the while. "Now, what is it you need? I may have some spares to give you, but we'll have to make the rest, maybe even find a crafting corner for larger batches."

"The usual," they said. "Healing, mana, poisons, and a few others. I picked up some new recipes, actually."

"Oh?" She glanced over her shoulder. "Do tell!"

"Burn cream, water breathing potions, eye drops, anti-poisons, sleeping potions—"

"That's quite the tall order, Meike." She leaned on the counter, softly humming to herself. "Some of which I'd have to special order. Water breathing potions require algae and seaweed as ingredients. A sleeping potion is as simple as mixing chamomile tea with more potent herbs, but application is a major factor."

"I wouldn't be using it on people," they said. "Just monsters."

"Oh, I'm not doubting you. It's a delicate balance, is all." She turned and placed her back to the counter, arms crossed as she examined Meike from head to toe. "Leave the water breathing potions and eye drops to me. Burn cream is something you can easily make on your own, but I'll help with the rest."

"I appreciate it," they said. "You've done so much for me, but I—"

She poked their cheek. "I do this because I want to. We have to stick together—as crafters and kinfolk."

"Kinfolk..."

"Come on, let's grab a spot while we can."

While it was often crowded and much too loud for their liking, the Crafter's Corner was *the* place to be. Freely available pots, clay, and other tools and materials for the struggling or frugal crafter. All thanks to the generosity of guilds and unaffiliated contributors.

It was all thanks to them that Meike had a proper sized cauldron for their potions. They peered into it now, mystified by the sheer amount produced by a few herbs and a hefty dose of water. "Wow, there's so much...do you think I'll be able to carry all of this?"

Moira peered into the pot with a frown. "Good question. You have a bag, right?"

They had *a* bag, but it wasn't big enough to lug around the thirty plus potions they expected. "It's not very sturdy," they said. "I'll have to make several trips until I can find something better."

"You don't have a proper rucksack? Meike, how do you normally carry your goods?"

Meike silently held up their bag, a simple leather bag with signs of wear and tear. Like many things, it was on their long list of upgrades, but continued to slip further and further down in priority.

"Hm, not bad if you're just carrying herbs and salves, but you need something that'll protect the containers."

"What do you recommend? Or who, really. I don't know who to go to for these things."

"I have a spare bag you can have. I haven't used it in a few years now, I think."

"Really? After you gave me your AC?"

"It's no big deal, Meike. If not you, I'd give it to someone else." She lowered her eyes, smiling as she admired the cooling potion. "And I'd rather it be you."

"You're really nice," they said, offering a broad smile of their own.

"I'm nice to *you*." She sighed and rocked back on her heels. "I'll send Effie to retrieve it for me. Let's get started on bottling, shall we?"

Meike groaned, but they were actually excited for this part of the process. It was time consuming and tedious work, but there was something satisfying about rationing the fluids out.

They'd been at this all morning, starting first with the inspection and preparation of herbs. Moira moved like Maggie, chopping and dicing with such speed and efficiency it left them dizzy; they were still mixing herbs while she got started on the eye drops. She similarly whipped up a small batch of water breathing potions as Meike rationed out tea leaves.

"I don't know if Ma—Ms. Blum has told you this, but there's more to healing than potions or even healing magic."

"Like what?" There was a lot Maggie hadn't told them; it was a game to her, it seemed.

"It's a bit...no, it's a very involved process. It requires an oven or the summer sun." She glanced outside. "And that time has come and gone..."

Summer...that's when it all changed for Meike. It was late September, maybe even October, by their watch. The winter months worried them the most, but they planned to be back in Laeford before the snow fell.

"Well, what is it?"

"Tablets," she said. "Little pills that pack more healing power than a simple drop of any potion."

"If that's true, then why aren't we making those? Why aren't you?"

"That's a question that's been rattling around for years now."

Meike admired the potion warming in their palm and set it aside with the others. "Where I'm from, we'd blame capitalism and corporate greed. I was hoping things were different here."

"Greed plagues us all, doesn't it?" Moira swished the ladle around in the pot and came up with a heaping scoop. She carefully poured it into the funnel, and down it went into a bottle. She moved with ease, not sparing a drop, and moved to the next bottle. "Greed and nostalgia, is what it is. But not everyone has access to stoves, either."

"Did they spread propaganda, too?"

"Yup...you should come to the convention next spring. The alchemy and herbalist guilds meet up once a month to discuss business and innovations. With alchemy it's very tech based, but occasionally potions come up. The kind that can..." She glanced around the area, but it was just the two of them in this corner. "Revive."

"Like—"

"You still have that potion I gave you, right?"

"Of course. I don't want to have to use it."

"Good. Keep it that way. But as I was saying, you should consider joining a guild. If not for herbalists, adventuring."

The pot was getting lower and lower, and soon it would be time to switch over. "Were you ever in one?"

"In the past. Today I stick with crafting and research guilds. It's nice. You meet all kinds of people there, and I'm even in a few secret projects."

"Any you can tell me about?"

"Nope! Top secret. But you're going to love it."

"I got everything you requested," Meike said, hyperaware of the potions in their bag—*Moira's* bag. Unlike theirs, Moira's didn't shuffle the containers around. Each potion had its own slot, much like Teddy's coat of vials. The only con was the size of the bag, which Meike carried on their back.

"In that little bag?"

"Ha ha. I have a second batch coming, but these are all for you."

"Ooh...that's not small at all, then." Anniken reached for it, but Meike shuffled back.

"You don't need them right away, do you?"

"I just want to see, Meike. I'm curious."

"Let me do it, then." They were indoors, otherwise Meike would've refused. "Forty healing potions in total, but I only have twenty here." They took out ten for Anniken, along with two water breathing potions, five vials of poison, the eye drops, and five sleeping potions. "I made extra poisons for Cass and Pickles, but the healing potions are split evenly."

"Oh, this is super! I'm going to let loose—within reason, of course."

"And my outfit?"

"I've got your poncho." She smirked. "And the little request you made." Anniken handed over the bundle of clothes, wrapped in the restored poncho. "Do you want to try them on?"

Meike threw off one end of the poncho, chest swelling with excitement. Leather. Red leather. They took out the jacket and admired the hand stitched material. On the front were the words NEO-TOKYO, A.D. 2019, in bold lettering. The back contained a large blue and red pill. Surrounding it was the phrase GOOD FOR HEALTH, BAD FOR EDUCATION. Anniken left her signature, a little Z, on the breast pocket.

"It's beautiful," they whispered.

"There's a t-shirt and some cargo pants, too. I figured an herbalist could use some extra potion holders.

"I'll try them on later, but I think they'll fit." The pants looked baggy enough to sit comfortably.

"Just try anyway, and let me know how they feel before we head out. It'll save us both time."

Meike tried on the jacket and marveled at the weight and feel of it. Like it just came off the rack... "I'm not going to wear it right away, but I think it would be nice to dress casually while we aren't questing."

"Good idea." She tucked the potions into her bag, a series of uneven clinking. "And just so you know, Cass is serving dinner out in the pavilion tonight."

"Do you think she'd mine if I invited a friend?"

"A friend, huh?" Anniken's eyes narrowed. "Are they a special kind of friend?"

"I sure hope so...Moira's really nice. She helped me with the potions and your eye drops."

"Did she, now?" Anniken chuckled to herself, laughing at an inside joke Meike wasn't privy to. "I'm sure Cass won't complain."

2

GOOD COMPANY

"You're inviting me to dinner?" Moira smiled, eyes demurely lowered. "I didn't think you were this bold, Meike."

"Huh? It's just a small thing my adventuring group is putting together. I wanted to treat you for helping me out recently."

"Right. Not a date." She winked. "And don't think I've forgotten about Vivica."

"I was hoping we could try now. Don't wanna do it on a full stomach, ya know?"

"That's fair, but are you sure you're up for it?"

Meike squared their shoulders beneath the new leather jacket. They never felt cool before, but that changed with this jacket. "I've never been more ready!" They even practiced beforehand and had the entire chant memorized front to back.

"Let's get her out, then!"

The extended stay did wonders for Vivica's temperament. She strolled into the center of the pentagram, the fur on her back and tail bristling, and flashed her teeth at Meike. It warranted a small nod of acknowledgment, but nothing more.

"I bind you," they said, projecting their voice over the ensuing breeze. Much like before, purple tendrils crept from the symbol and attached themselves to the wolf. "I bind you to the token. Under my service, forever, until we part."

Vivica bowed her head, tail thrashing from side to side as Meike completed the chat. The wolf shaped token jolted onto its front paws. Her eyes flashed, as did those of the token.

Moira silently urged them on, her eyes bright and sharp, the words poised on her lips.

"I bind you, Vivica!" A slap of the foot punctuated that last beat, and Vivica threw her head back in a soundless howl, her body warping and winding into the tiny figure.

The token threw itself every which way, and several times Meike noted the snarling wolf inside, just dying to be let out. And then the token rattled to a stop, its eyes haunted by a pale blue light.

"Well done," Moira said, politely clapping. "It went off without a hitch!"

"For now," they said, the token burning a pattern into their hand. The previous marks from Alek's were mostly healed. "I still have to let her out later."

"It gets easier over time. She may retain some hostility after—Vivica isn't a proper summon, like Effie."

"Did Effie ever…" They jostled the token from hand to hand. Rather than cool down, it continued to heat up; Vivica's last attempt at rebellion. "…break free?"

Moira smirked. "Tried, in the beginning. But demons are held to higher standards than tamed beasts. Once they're bound to us, they obey regardless of personal preferences."

"No free will, then?"

"It's dangerous in the wrong hands. But they're guaranteed to not turn on you, either. Well…"

"What?"

"It's…it's complicated." She paced around the pentagram, wary of its smudged edges. "A weak mage has no hope of corralling a strong demon. Some have tried in the past, only to be devoured at the first misstep. That initial union is important." She clenched and unclenched her hand as she spoke. "If it senses even the slightest bit of weakness, the demon will continue to test you in small ways."

"So it's not enough to beat them, you have to earn their respect?" That seemed too much of a gamble to Meike, and far worse, if anything.

"Think of it as a gap in armor. One thrust is all it takes to fell even the greatest of warriors."

"That sounds…exhausting. I think I'll take my chances with beasts and monsters."

"Don't give up so soon! You can always try when you're stronger. I wouldn't recommend anything stronger than an imp at your current level, but maybe in the future…"

"When I've gained enough strength and respect, yes." Meike tucked the token in the leather pouch attached to their belt. "For now, I just wanna eat. Do you need time to get ready?"

"Sure, give me ten minutes to freshen up."

She said ten, but it took closer to twenty-five. But Meike couldn't complain, despite being forced to wait outside. "I don't have a lot of privacy, as you can see," she said with a nervous chuckle.

Moira swapped out her standard robes for a soft green tunic and leggings, with some rather lovely boots. She'd taken some time to craft herself a flower crown and touched up her makeup. Perhaps it was the latter that lit her up, highlighting the dimples in her chin, and her warm brown eyes. Or was it the shy smile she wore now, going wide when Meike stopped to observe.

"Sorry for making you wait," she said, taking their arm. "I hope we aren't too late."

"No, you're fine," they murmured, feeling wildly out of touch with the stunning Moira at their side. People up and down the street paused to stare, and Meike timidly hid their face in her shoulder.

"Oi, Meike!" Pickles greeted them first, his tail wagging from side to side. "I didn't know we were allowed to bring a date."

"She's not my—"

"We're just *very* good friends," Moira said.

"Sure, friends." Pickles winked. "Just one step away from be-ing...*roommates*." He broke out in laughter, and Moira politely chuckled, but Meike didn't see what all the fuss was about.

"Moira, this is Pickles. The other two are Anniken and Cass."

"Aw, what a sweet boy," she cooed, stooping to pet Pickles and give him scritches. He was far kinder to her than Anniken, tail wagging as he allowed himself to be fawned over.

They turned to Cass, who maintained her distance. "What are we having?"

"Enough food for everyone, I hope." She sighed and handed them two plates. "One for you and your date. I made several small pies for everyone. Vegetarian for you, of course. There's also salad and soup. Nothing glamorous, but the meat pies contain lamb and chicken, depending on your fancy," she said to Moira.

"Hard choice, but I think I'll go with lamb."

"Excellent choice! It's expensive, but I love the taste of lamb."

"Moira, is it?" Anniken broke her pie in half, revealing a chunk of meat and thickened broth. "How'd you two meet?"

"We bumped into each other while on the job. Isn't that right, Meike?"

"Yes...over by the docks." They also met Patches that day, but Moira...she was something else. Kinfolk.

Anniken chewed on her food, seemingly content by that answer.

"I don't know if Meike's told you, but I work part time as an herbalist. My true passion lies in alchemy."

"Alchemy," Cass exclaimed. "Have you worked on any interesting projects lately?"

"Several, actually. I can't say what in particular, but it's big." She spread her hands in the air. "Keep an eye on the news—it's going to be huge! Innovative."

"You can't spare a little hint?"

"Sorry! I gave the guild my word." She winked. "But you're going to love it!"

"Is it something we can all use? Or is it adventurer specific?"

"For everyone! But please don't ask me for more."

"I've got theories of my own," Anniken said. "But I can respect a non-disclosure agreement. And besides, this is a celebration."

"Right," Meike said, thankful for the change in topic. "We'll be traveling for the next two months. There's still a few things I'd like, but that can wait."

"We're going to clear out that old mine. Other groups have tried in the past, but those damn vermin keep coming back."

"Of course they come back," Cass said. "There's no one there to defend it or the potential miners."

The conversation quickly veered into politics, and the lax care of the country's outskirts. According to Cass, the Silverstone Mine used to be quite robust, and the town of Ashford held in great esteem for its silver veins and exports. But that was several decades ago, before the veins supposedly went dry. It was a gradual process, with shipments fewer and fewer, until one day there was simply nothing left to give.

"But that doesn't make sense," Meike said. "I thought it was closed from the kobold infestation and negligence of the—."

"Careful," Cass said, glancing at Anniken. "The Queen has eyes and ears beyond the castle walls."

"I certainly hope you aren't accusing me of anything," Anniken quietly said, the lower half of her face hidden behind her cup.

"No, but I hadn't forgotten your affiliation with a certain...Knight."

The air between the two women crackled like lightning, but it was Pickles who broke the silence.

"That's all they are, Cass. Rumors. No one knows what happened at Ashfort, but it wasn't abandoned because the mines were empty."

She sighed and refilled her cup—wine. Meike was the only one drinking water tonight. "Then please, dog. Enlighten us."

"You saw that old quest a while ago, with the group who wanted to go in and clean up," Pickles said, more to Meike than the rest of the group. "The mine's overrun with kobolds and other monsters by now, I'm sure. Like trolls."

Meike shifted in their seat and lowered their gaze to the cooling pie on their plate. That sounded vaguely familiar, like something they read about during their first day in Laeford. The request echoed many starter dungeons in so many MMOs Meike played in their youth. Kobolds were the lowest of the low, after all. They tore into their pie as Pickles continued.

"Some thirty or forty years ago, the town of Ashfort changed hands, from the kindly mayor to a stern penny pincher..."

They had a good idea already of how things transpired, but Meike remained silent. Anniken looked up from her food to watch Pickles with sharp eyes.

"Wally Culthapp retired to be with his daughter and her family in a city outside of the country. He was a good man, who always looked out for his people—especially the miners. He had a few enemies by way of overseers and business-men—you know the sort."

"Aye," Cass said. "He had a good heart, that one."

"The new mayor, Steven Robert, was voted in with dirty money. The townspeople were pressured by his hired goons. A few dissenting farmers lost livestock. Others got roughed up. At the face level, Steve was a charismatic and soft spoken fellow. Unable or unwilling to fight back, the town went on as if Culthapp never left. Until Steve gradually increased taxes."

"And the ones at the bottom felt it first," Anniken said. "But the middle class and up didn't feel the true strain of it until egg and milk prices doubled."

"That's it," Pickles said. "Miners got the worse of it. Stevie boy wanted to double their output, and trade with outside vendors and countries. He ran them ragged, demanding they work longer shifts and dig deeper, always deeper. Thought that maybe there was some gold hidden in that old mine."

"Oh no," Meike murmured.

"Yeah." He licked his nose. "So, the mine collapsed, killing dozens of miners. The ones that weren't crushed were trapped inside, where they slowly wasted away, waiting for help that never came."

"Dead miners, poor excavation, and..." Anniken chewed on the last of her pie. "Let me guess, they ran the mayor out of town?"

"Worse than that, actually. He raided the town treasury and ran off before the people could grab their pitchforks."

"Typical man," Cass said, lip curled. "I hope he got everything he deserved."

"He did. A bounty hunter dragged him to the capital, where he was hanged."

"Oh," she said, slowly blinking. "Good riddance."

"He had many offenses under his belt, but I think abandoning a town in need was the final straw." Pickles grinned. "That, and tax evasion."

"That's horrible," Moira said. "But what became of Ashfort?"

"A replacement was sent to govern, a mindless plant who did as his handlers instructed. Ashfort quickly fell into decline—there were better mines, and that area has always given travelers trouble. Without proper guards to keep out the riffraff, the people were left to fend for themselves."

"That can't be all, can it?"

"It's basically a ghost town. The only people still there are the stubborn or those with little prospects elsewhere." He dunked his muzzle into his cup and drank long and deep, and came up with wine clinging to his fur. "Not worth leaving without a horse or a sword."

Anniken set her cup down with a heavy thud. "Is it even worth saving? If the Queen doesn't care about it, why should we?"

"I don't see why not," Moira said. "It's in the perfect spot for a trade route. It just needs to be properly maintained—build a garrison, stock it with soldiers, and clear the mountains of monsters."

"That's a tall ask, and we're just four people—"

"Doesn't have to be that way," Cass said. "There are other options."

Silence fell once more as the two women sized each other up. Anniken stood abruptly and leaned against the table, shaking it in the process. She opened her mouth, face flushed with too much wine and excitement. "Ah, do what you like!" She shoved her chair aside and stormed off into a side alley.

Pickles barked after her, but she paid him no mind. "What's eating her?"

"Hmph, who knows? But I hope she fixes that attitude soon." Cass fussed over the leftovers. There were a few pies left, but nothing Meike cared to eat. "Moira, it was lovely meeting you, but I'm going to retire for the night. Meike and Pickles...I'll see you two later."

Without Cass or Anniken to field questions, Meike found themself fidgeting and wanting to puncture the silence. They had questions of their own about the mine and the neighboring town. There was so much to process, and they couldn't help but wonder if Pickles hadn't made the whole thing up—or fibbed a little.

Moira politely coughed into her hand. "I should be going, too. I have an early day tomorrow and need to work the wine out of my system. Meike?"

"Huh?"

She stood before them, hand shyly extended. "Do you want to walk me home?"

"Why" formed on their lips, but a soft growl from Pickles set them in action. "Of course," Meike said, taking her arm. Never mind that they wanted to hurry to their room and get some sleep themself, but...

"I had a lot of fun," she said, oddly subdued. "I don't believe half the things he said about Ashfort, but there's some truth to it."

"Such as?"

"Bad leadership and the mine's collapse. No one doubts that, but all that nonsense about bribes and cattle killers...that's all window dressing, Meike."

The streets weren't quite empty, but lacked the usual hustle and bustle of the day. Most people were safely tucked indoors or on their way home. Those who loitered in the shadows, just outside the dim light radiating from lamp posts, watched the hurried pair with hungry eyes. The sword on Meike's hip was a cold comfort; if one wanted it badly enough, it wouldn't be hard to disarm them and turn the blade.

"I'll find out," they said, voice deepening as they glared at a would-be pickpocket. The scoundrel sulked off, but Meike kept an eye on him as they walked Moira to her apartment. The front entrance glowed with a warm light, a beacon to them and an alarm to intruders.

"Do let me know what you find," Moira said, lingering in the doorway. "And Meike?"

"Yes?" Without her at their side, a coldness crept into their limbs. They placed a reassuring hand not on their sword, but on the pouch containing their familiars.

"Be careful. And don't forget to write."

3

Walk A Mile In My Shoes

"It's your first time in the capital, isn't it?"

She alone was to blame for the delay in acquiring a horse, but Anniken had a lot on her mind recently. None of that concerned Silverstone, what she considered a simple dungeon clear. A ragtag bunch of kobolds and the occasional troll was no match for her yet to be named blade. Meike, however...

"Yup," they said, tightening their arm around Anniken's waist as Vallens eased into a trot. Meike had a talent for being distracted, this time by their new AC. It was a curious device, closer to a toy. They played a game of sorts on it for the past few hours.

"Would you put that away for five minutes and talk to me? I'm not your chauffeur."

Cass had a horse of her own, and a sidesaddle for Pickles to ride in. The damn mutt argued to run free, but acquiesced when put to reason. He had no hope of keeping up with the horses, at least not at a comfortable gait.

"Sorry," they mumbled, and tucked the device away. "I'm still learning. The range is poor, but I can browse the Board from here."

"In Laeford? I doubt there's anything good there. You'll want to leave space for the real quests in Redadore."

"Redadore," they said, a soft murmur lost among the beating of hooves and the dog's raucous laughter.

Anniken caught a snatch of the exchange between him and Cass—some vulgar song he picked up from his brief stint as a sailor. Now *there* was a creature who lived, truly lived, but on his terms alone, traveling far and wide, while holding tight to his secrets.

"It's beautiful. You're sure to love it, but try not to get too attached. We're only stopping by for two things."

"The horse and fresh supplies."

"Good. But you're forgetting something..."

"Laken?"

"Yeah." A hard knot formed in the pit of her stomach. Laken... She'd reached out to them last night, not by PDA, but pigeon. It was faster that way. Mana wasn't quite strong enough to transport messages at the snap of a finger, and she'd heard of them failing. Pigeon just seemed like the safer bet.

It was brief, perhaps for the sake of Anniken's pride, but Meike hugged her tight. They uttered no platitudes or apology, but settled into idle chatter about the passing foliage.

They were an odd one, but sometimes Meike was rather nice to have around. And not just for their potions.

"What's it like?"

"...Sorry, what?"

"The *capital*," they said, digging their short nails into Anniken's tunic. "Do they have an elaborate rose garden?"

"Roses? I suppose, but I don't know why you're interested in that, of all things."

"Just preparing myself for the reveal, is all." Their tone took on a dreamy quality. "I wonder if there's a maze..."

"Oh, now you're just being silly. But it is rather beautiful. Or so I've been told, anyway." Laken promised to take her once, but between their knightly obligations, and Anniken's thirst for adventure, there simply wasn't time.

But Laken found time to acquire a preserved rose, clipped by the Queen's very own gardener. Deep crimson with the thorns carefully extracted...

Her hands tightened around the reins as Meike squealed and pointed at the first magnificent spire poking above the treeline.

"Yeah, that's it. That's Redadore." Named for being the most beloved city in the land, and for the red clay that made up its buildings and streets. Laeford may have been a labor of love, but Redadore was a work of art.

According to the poets who loitered about and boasted its beauty.

She was free to roll her eyes for now, but adapted a neutral expression as the guards greeted them.

"What business have you in these parts," the man bellowed, hand on his spear. His fellow watched in silence, daring them to make one wrong move.

Anniken waved for the group to remain silent. "We're just travelers, in need of provisions and lodging for the night."

The talkative one spat to the side and approached first Anniken, then Cass. "Three of ya, is it?" He shoved his hand into Pickles' face. "Here's a good boy, is he? Want some jerky, little fella?" He prodded Pickles' nose with the back of his hand and gave him a rough scratch behind the ear. "Dodgy one, huh? Don't blame him!"

"Can we go? I'd like to have my affairs settled before dark."

"Yeah yeah, get on with ya!" He rapped the butt of his spear on the ground. "You aren't the only travelers on this here road."

"Fuck you," Pickles growled as they stepped into the city proper. "What's with men thinking they can handle beasts as they please?"

"It's because they see anything 'lesser' than themselves as exploitable," Cass said.

"No shit. I want out of this bag," he said, squirming.

"Hold on, Pickles! Let's find a stable first."

Anniken let out a sharp whistle. "Quiet down, both of you, and follow me. Trust me when I say you don't want to be stabled *here*."

"I'll take your word for it, though I've been to this city countless times," Cass said with a sniff. "More than you, I'm sure."

"Please don't make a scene," she snapped, urging Vallens down the street.

The downside to large cities like these was how crowded they were, especially at the height of day. It was worse in the morning, when everyone was going to and from the market and other hot spots. A few now were hurrying along, arms or carts laden with food, supplies, and other odds and ends. Spotting the tourists and travelers came easy to her now; they were the ones who leisurely strolled about, eyes and mouths wide in astonishment, and it wouldn't surprise her if Meike responded in kind. But she couldn't blame them, either; it was intoxicating.

The red bricked buildings had a modern edge to them, boasting the wealth and status of the city. The corner shops and salespersons would fit right at home back on Earth, minus the obvious technological advancements. But even here they had comparable amenities, such as running water, mana powered stoves, *bidets*...and little computer-like devices, not quite laptops or phones, but close enough it gave her a shock to see. Laken teased her for it then, and the memory brought a blush to her cheeks.

She hoped to run into them...

"We're stopping here?" The despair in Cass' tone was not lost on her, slight as it was. "I don't think..."

"It's fine." Anniken dismounted and helped Meike down. "It's not just for knights and nobles." She handed the reins over to the stable lad, who was dressed far better and cleaner than some of the stable hands found in Laeford. "His name is Val-lens. Please take good care of him."

"Naturally," he said, with that strong Redadore accent. "Jennings will see to your friend's horse." He offered a deep bow before leading the horse into an empty stall.

"I never would've guessed," Cass said. She stuck an arm into the air, and that foul-mouthed heron of hers fluttered down and perched on her shoulder. "See? That wasn't so bad, was it?"

Pickles scratched himself behind the ear, notably in the same spot the guard handled. "So what's on the agenda for today?"

"We're here for provisions and a horse for Meike. I want you to keep that in mind, when you're out running with the local mutts. I'd like to set out before the sun rises."

"Why so early? Don't you wanna take in the city and take leisurely bubble baths?"

Cass hummed to herself, stroking her cheek. "I do love a good bath."

"You're free to do as you please once we're all stocked up."

"Yes, let us handle Meike and our supplies, while you run off with your beau."

Anniken grit her teeth, painfully aware of the heat in her cheeks, and the rage simmering just below. "You should be grateful I'm even bothering."

The tavern was dark and crowded, clouds of smoke curling from the booths in the back. A serving girl danced from table to table, deftly evading broad, calloused hands, two drink laden trays in each hand. Despite her full figure, she easily made room for Anniken in the narrow walkway.

"Need anything, Miss?" She fetched a pad and a piece of charcoal from her apron. "Spiced peach tea, 'haps?"

"I'd like a plum brandy, actually." She nodded at a booth furthest from the door, thinly veiled by a cloak hanging from above. A black cloak, reversed and hiding the queen's sigil. The red rose Anniken knew all too well...

The server lowered her voice, ignoring the din of rowdy customers. "Don't go messin' where you don't belong, now."

"It's alright. They're expecting me."

She stepped around the quietly gasping woman and took one last deep breath before braving the fog of pipe smoke. Somehow it smelled worse than weed, and even breathing through her mouth wasn't enough to save her.

Anniken let out a slight cough, felt the burning in her chest, and sank into the open seat at the booth. "I knew I'd find you here."

"I know. Why do you think I mentioned the name to you?" Laken briefly lifted the cap from their head, revealing their cool blue eyes, and the standard braid encircling their head like a crown.

To see them now, that devilish smile and handsome countenance and build...Anniken dug her nails into the palms of her hands, the sharp pain grounding her back in reality. Laken was very attractive, yes, and she was lucky to have their full attention—

"Here's your brandy, Miss!"

Anniken snapped back just as the server arrived, a strained smile on her face, with not one but two drinks.

"I only asked for the one—"

"And for you, Ser." She gave a light curtsy, mindful of the prying eyes. "Please call if there's anything more you need."

"That'll be all, Matilda. Thank you."

Matilda giggled and hurried off, hips swaying from side to side.

"Hmph. A bit too friendly, isn't she?"

"It's not like you to get jealous, Zel." The soft purr in their voice aroused something within her. Mostly rage, but at least 10% of that was lust.

"I'm not jealous. I just—"

"Don't like when other women take notice of me?" They weren't smiling now, but Anniken liked that even less. That placid expression may as well have been reserved for a lowly insect. "I can't help it that people find me attractive, Zelamir."

"No," she said, steadying her shaking hands. "But you can choose whether or not to act on it."

"Good grief." Laken lowered that awful hat, a toque over their eyes. "I didn't come here to argue, as I assumed of you."

"And I didn't come here for a fight, so don't push me."

"Your brazenness is what I like about you. Now, tell me about this request?"

Finally, they could get back to the matter at hand. "It's about the Silverstone Mine. Me and my colleagues plan on liberating it from the monsters infesting it and the neighboring town."

"Ashfort." Their lip curled in distaste. "It's not worth saving. There's nothing of value, otherwise we would've done so long ago."

"Really, now? How much do you really know?"

"As much as the Queen permits." Laken squeezed the handle of their tankard. Knowing them, it was likely a grain-based ale. Beer was disgusting, but some people chose to drink it, anyway. "I can't imagine someone of your standing is in a position to know more."

"Maybe. Maybe not." Anniken sipped at her own drink and frowned. It was more bitter than sweet, and not in the pleasant way of citrus. "We'll uncover the secrets of the mine, but we're going to need someone to maintain its security."

"And you expect the Queen—Queen Illora—to spare a knight or two for a defunct mine?" Chuckling, they brought the mug to their lips and drained half of it in one go. "You'll have better luck drawing blood from a stone."

"It lies on a valuable trade route. Why wouldn't you want to save it?"

"That's a very astute question." Laken's tankard dully clunked against the tabletop. "I could argue your case to the Queen, but I can't guarantee anything."

"Understandable, but I would appreciate you trying." While easily swayed by the pleasures of the flesh, Laken had some integrity. She was reliable when it came to her duties, too…

And now she was walking her hand across the table, long fingers reaching for Anniken's hand…

But it was Laken whose wrist was secured, not the other way around. Anniken squeezed it now, admiring the pulse beneath her thumb.

"You don't get to do that," she said, not caring if anyone saw. "Not after what you did to me."

"Zel—"

"No." She released them with a light flick. "I'm not ready for that talk now, and I don't know if I ever will be. I need my space, understand?"

Laken huffed over her ale, eyes deliberately skewed to the left. "I'm sorry. I really am."

"Don't," she snarled. "Facta, non verba."

"There you go again, in that strange language of yours."

"It's not strange. It's Latin. Actions, not words."

"I see." Laken's eyes lowered, fixated on the dregs of her beer. "I'll just have to prove it to you, then."

Anniken grimaced at her cup, more than half full with the bitter liquid. But if Laken could do it…so could she. "Focus on establishing a guard, and then we'll talk."

"Zelamir."

She shook her head, mind made up, and tilted her head back to accommodate the heft of the tankard. It was awful, all of it, but Anniken choked down the brandy and slammed her empty cup on the table.

"I expect to hear back from you in a week's time," she said, rising unsteadily to her feet. The rush of liquor weighed heavily on her mind, but she felt on top of the world.

4

BUTTERSCOTCH

Were it not for Cass' guidance, Meike would happily wander the streets of Redadore. There was so much to do, so much to see! And oh, how they longed to browse one of the many bookshops! Used, new, fiction, and non!

But Cass had a tight grip on their collar, and Pickles nearly tripped them. Not on purpose (or so they thought), but supposedly because he saw a pretty dog. The timing sure was convenient...

"Keep it together, Meike. We're here on business, not pleasure."

"Wasn't it you who mentioned the bathhouses?"

"So I did," she said quietly. "You would too, if you only knew what you were missing."

"What *am* I missing?" Before coming to Glasend, the only bathhouses they knew of were depictions in anime, and the scant idea of baths in New York.

Giant hot baths, yay.

Cass sighed deeply, a flicker of despair in her eyes. "Oh you sweet, innocent child...words alone cannot do it justice!"

"If you say so." They wouldn't mind going for a dip. It had been...too long since they last had a proper bath. And as someone who always preferred brisk showers to soaking in their own filth, they would kill for a bath.

"I *know* so," Cass said, huffing. She steered Meike away from a group of performers, and onto a less crowded street.

Small shops and restaurants lined either side, and there was no shortage of samples and leaflets.

"Oi. Back off, all of you," Pickles barked when Meike started to get overwhelmed. "I fucking hate being a tourist."

"You and me both," Meike said. They massaged their forehead. Being in new environments always ran the risk of overstimulation, but it was usually worth it.

They drifted further from the heart of the city, past a residential area, and into the market square.

With stalls as far as the eye could see, Redadore's market put Laeford to shame. Meike stopped to gape at a horse-sized statue of a dragon, carved in marble. It had two glittering gems for eyes, and a snarling jaw lit with flames.

"Come on, Meike!" Cass yanked them away before the shopkeeper got a word in edge-wise. She wouldn't even let them admire the winged pig in a too small cage! Poor thing barely had room to turn around.

It wasn't until they reached their destination that Meike noticed Pickles was missing. Probably chasing another girl dog or begging for scraps.

"Good day," the deeply tanned man before them said. His hair was gray at the temples, and he wore a simple stained tunic. Meike almost mistook him for a humble farmer, except he wasn't surrounded by ears of corn or baskets of apples. Looming behind him was a small stable and the smell of barn animals.

"Hello there," Cass said. "We're in the market for a horse."

"So you are! For you or the little one here?"

"Hey!" They were a little on the short side, but they weren't a *child*.

"Is for horses," Cass said, gently pinching Meike's arm. "I already have a horse, but they could use one. What do you recommend?"

"That depends on what you need the horse for. Standard traffic, or something more robust?"

"We're heading towards the mountains, so anything that's strong enough for that."

"Ahh, I have just the steed for you!"

He brought out a tall, handsome horse with pitch-black fur. "If you're headed out towards the mountains, you're going to want a strong and sure footed horse, like my dear Sebastian."

Sebastian lowered his head and gently neighed. His warm brown eyes encouraged Meike to step forward and pet him. How long had he been back here, waiting for someone to come and adopt him?

"My, he seems to have taken a liking to you! Would you like to take him for a ride?"

Cass cleared her throat. "He is a lovely horse, but I don't think he's Meike's *speed*."

"But Sebastian is my best horse! People flock from all corners of the country to assess his strength and beauty."

"And I don't doubt that," she said evenly. "But I believe this fine horse is out of our budget."

He coughed. "Well, I have a deal just for you—"

"What other horses do you have?"

Meike bade a silent farewell to the beautiful black stallion. The other stallions, all proud and lovely horses, lacked Sebastian's composure. One even snorted and tried to bite them!

"I don't think any of these are a good fit for me," Meike said, defeated. "How much is Sebastian?"

But before the man could talk up his prized steed, Cass took the reins. "What about that pony in the corner?"

His face fell. "I've had that old pony for a few years now. No one wants him because he's a stubborn as a mule."

Cass glanced at Meike, the smallest of smiles on her face. "Bring him out. Meike here is good with animals."

But not with horses and ponies, they wanted to argue. They could surely work out a deal with the man for Sebastian. How much could he cost?

The pony ambled out of the stall, taking a moment to nibble on a stray patch of grass. His handler grunted in disdain. "You see this? He has no respect for time. No, trust me when I say you don't want him leading you through treacherous terrains! You want a good, sturdy horse like my Sebastian." He pounded his chest.

Meike cautiously approached the pony, expecting another nip. But the pretty pony, with its caramel fur and honey colored mane, calmly sniffed their hand. He blinked at them, and without warning, shoved his head into their hand.

They giggled and combed through his mane as the pony teased them like a giant puppy. He licked their hand and curiously nibbled on the hem of their poncho. "I'll take him!"

Cass beamed at the man, her teeth smaller and not as impressive as any horse, but just as fierce. "You heard them. What's your price?"

He sighed and shook his head. "Five gold, but don't say I didn't warn you."

Still giggling, Meike hugged the pony's broad neck. "Does he have a name? Cause I think he looks like a Butterscotch!"

"I called him Albert, but he never responded to it. Like I said, he's a very stubborn creature. Ponies are harder to work with."

He said that, but Butterscotch rested his neck on Meike's shoulder, neighing loudly in their ear. Butterscotch wasn't as graceful as the stately Sebastian, but he was just as affectionate and deserving of love as anyone.

"You named it Butterscotch?" Anniken wasn't too impressed by the pony, which was clear by her exasperated tone, but Meike was too happy to let her dampen their spirits.

"Yeah," they said, lovingly brushing the pony's honey colored mane. "He's a sweetheart."

"Whatever," she said, stroking the pony's nose. It closed its eyes and leaned into it. Behind her, Vallens huffed and turned his head. He was very prideful for a horse, one born and reared for ferrying passengers. "How much did you pay for it?"

"Five gold. I used the rest of the money to buy extra rations. I figured you didn't want the change."

"I don't. We'll make that back and triple, by the time we're done with the mine."

"And how did—"

She turned so sharply, eyes filled with quiet fury, that Meike shrank back into the comfort of Butterscotch's stocky frame.

"Forget I said anything." They just wanted to know if she patched things up with Laken or not.

Cass was bolder, but she played it safe. "Do we have clearance or not?"

"Laken said she'd handle it, assuming we hold up our end of the bargain. I told her to give us a week at the most."

"Is that it?"

"For now. The only stipulation is that we have to hold down the fort until the guard arrives, but that'll give us time to count our spoils."

Spoils! Meike hummed to themself, eager to get started right away. Anxiety bubbled just below the surface, but they could fret over that later. What mattered now was the journey, and with such a strong crew around them, the odds of failing were slim.

"Now, where's that dog?"

Pickles poked his nose from Cass' saddlebag. "I'm waiting on you lot! I got all gussied up for this." It was true. He took a bath last night and allowed Meike to trim and brush his fur and tail. He looked quite handsome, a traveling scarf tied around his neck.

"And I see you have the heaviest bag among us," Anniken said, nodding at Butterscotch's heavy saddlebags.

"Butterscotch is strong enough to handle it. The seller said they're better than horses and as good as mules, if you want to haul a cart or heavy load." He tried to sell them a cart too, offering a deal of eight gold coins. If Cass hadn't shot him down (she was awfully fast, that one), Meike would've bought it. They weren't in the market for a cart, anyway.

"Ponies are? I never would've guessed..." Anniken dropped her eyes, an awkward smile briefly crossing her face. She wasn't always so quick to admit fault, so Meike naturally wondered if she was truly herself at the moment.

Or if she still had Laken on the mind.

Anniken retained some of her prickliness from the previous day, but something about her was different. She seemed happier, albeit troubled. Yet her steps were lighter, and Meike spotted a shy smile on her lips as their small procession funneled out of the city.

"How'd you find it," she said, once they were safely on the road.

They walked in single file, Vallens taking the lead, Butterscotch following close behind, and Cass' Jennie at the rear. Trees and bushes lined either side of the road, a hint of danger lurking just around the corner.

"Find what?"

"Redadore. Did you like it?"

Oh, that! "I love it! Had we not found Laeford first, I would love to stay there."

Laeford had its charm for sure, and they would miss their friends (Moira most of all), but Redadore had more libraries and specialty shops. And a massive building dedicated to guilds. Meike's time was precious, so they did little more than glance at the magnificent buildings. But they vowed to return and buy their weight in books and scrolls.

"I bet you would. Unlike Laeford, there are affordable apartments and houses. If you know where to look…"

"So it's the same, then?"

"Not quite," Cass cut in. "The housing market in Laeford is very competitive. Many people—crafters and common folk alike—go there for the salt air and quiet life."

"As quiet as you can get in a city," Pickles said. "And Redadore's nice if you're a tourist, but I wouldn't want to live there. I like Laeford."

"And in Redadore, you'll find more competition with more established herbalists. You may have to sell at a loss."

"I don't care about being a bigwig or making a lot of money. I just want to live peacefully and help those in need."

"That's mighty kind of you," Anniken said. "But you won't get far with that mindset." She lowered her voice. "This world is kinder than our own in many ways, but money is still king."

"But it doesn't have to be!"

While they couldn't live without, Meike got along well enough with the little they had. It was possible to live in relative comfort, doubly so if you knew how to farm or garden, and could afford a plot of land.

Someday they hoped to do so, and would be glad to share a home with Moira, if she wanted a change of scenery. There would be no fear of her plants being tossed from the roof, and she could have an extra room to herself for her research and crafting.

"Wouldn't you—"

"Careful," Pickles called out. "Cass, send out Jasper. I think we've got trouble ahead." He thumped onto the ground and dashed ahead, axe in mouth. "And you two, ready your weapons."

"And what about me?"

Pickles dropped the axe into his paw-like hands and rose onto his hind paws. "Just stay out of the way."

In the distance, a large figure blocked the path.

5

GOTTA PAY THE TROLL TOLL

Pickles charged ahead, while Jasper circled overhead. "Fall back," Cass said, urging her horse forward.

"But I can help," Meike protested.

Anniken glanced at them, face now partially obscured by a leather helm. "Meike, please! This could be serious. We don't have time to coddle you."

Coddle...

Being treated like a child hurt more than anything, but Meike kept silent as they rode along, allowing Butterscotch to lower its speed and make room for Cass and Anniken to walk abreast. It was difficult to make anything out from up ahead, with the two of them in the way, cloaks flapping in the breeze, hands on their respective weapons.

'I can help...'

Meike's hand moved not to their sword or newly crafted staff and grimoire, but to the pouch that housed their familiars. Saffron was obviously out, as was Alek, but Vivica...

"*Troll*," Pickles' voice rang out. "Troll on the bridge!"

Anniken and Cass slowed to a crawl, weapons out and at the ready. Meike bounced the wolf token in their palm, bracing one hand on the grimoire belted to their hip. This was it! Their first battle since stopping in Zachick.

Vallens moved to the side of the road, where he waited as Anniken dismounted and joined Pickles, who was brawling with the monster. Cass similarly steered Jennie out of danger's grasp, but didn't stray far from the horses. Instead, she lined up a shot, eyes narrowed and hand poised to let loose the arrow—once she had a good sight of the troll's weak spot.

And Meike...remained on their pony, conflicted on obeying orders or being a free spirit like Pickles.

It was also their first time seeing a troll in this world, and up close, at that! The monster was hideous and well over ten feet, wiry black hair covering its flat and elongated head, arms, and legs. It wore no clothing, other than a raggedy loin cloth that did little to hide its grotesque and inflamed genitalia. In its hands was a crude wooden club, which shook the ground each time he swung (and missed) at Pickles.

He wasn't quite on the bridge itself, a narrow structure made from clay and stone, and strayed further from it as Pickles danced around its ankles.

"Come on, you big smelly dolt!" Pickles artfully spun in the air as the troll's club thudded into the ground, narrowly missing his tail. "You can't catch me." He shook his butt, evoking a deep growl from the monster.

"Over here, Pickles," Anniken cried out, twirling her sword like a baseball bat. "Let's get this over with!"

"What a fowl creature...Anniken, step aside." Cass let fly a second later, and the arrow struck home in the troll's neck.

Meike glanced away as the troll groaned and pawed at the arrow. They didn't want to see the blood and gore, or its final moments. But the roar of anger and sounds of sword on thick flesh caught their attention. And there was Anniken, sawing into the flesh of its arm.

The troll snarled and dropped the club to grab her—a mistake that made Meike wince—and lost two fingers when Anniken countered.

"Oh, I hate trolls," Cass said, notching another arrow. "They aren't much trouble if you spot them first—" Her arrow tore into its shoulder, and she cursed. "Big, slow, and unintelligent creatures. Not much different from a giant in that regard, but I'd rather not come across one of those, either." She cheered when her third arrow pierced the troll's head.

Meike swayed slightly in their saddle. They swallowed the urge to vomit; to do so would cement their fate as a weakling, even if no one would dare say so aloud.

At least the troll was half-dead, tottering on unsteady legs red from fresh cuts and bites. Anniken and Pickles moved in tandem, one slashing and leaping back to allow the other to rush in and hack away. It was a lot like dancing, in a way; the two moved with perfect symmetry.

"Just one more..."

The troll stiffened as several arrows penetrated its chest in quick succession. Grinning wildly, Anniken turned her blade and sliced it from hip to sternum. It slumped heavily to the ground, jaw slack, and eyes glazed over.

Meike heaved a low sigh of relief. Finally, the nightmare was over. And under three minutes, by their estimate. It was scary how efficient their teammates could be.

"You really are an ugly brute," Anniken said, kicking the troll's lifeless body. She ripped off the coin purse attached to its hip and riffled through it, nodding in agreement at the contents. "I wonder how many people it killed to collect this much." She bounced the heavy bag in her palm. "We can sort this out later, when we settle down for the night."

"Just like that?" It was the first words they spoke since the fight began, and the words sounded painfully tiny to their ears.

"Well, we should probably clear the road first." Pickles sank his teeth into the troll's arm and tugged. The body followed seconds later, slow and heavy. But it was better than anything Meike could muster.

"Good idea," Anniken said, moving to assist him. With their combined strength, the troll was moved to the side of the road, among a patch of wildflowers and weeds. "There's a use for you in death and that's as fertilizer."

From the back of her horse, Cass cleared her throat. "You would think the Queen's men would guard this road carefully, considering its connection to the capital."

"It's not that close." Anniken spat on the troll, its body steaming and gradually congealing. "The guards don't patrol this area as heavily, unless their scouts detect imminent danger. But it's unusual for trolls and the like to be so bold."

"What's wrong with its body?" Meike pointed at the almost unrecognizable lump of flesh. Mundane beasts and other monsters didn't deteriorate nearly as fast as this one.

"That's normal for trolls, though I've heard of some monsters being reduced to stone or muck."

They had no choice but to believe her, for Anniken and the others clambered onto their respective mounts, eagerly chatting about their first troll encounters.

"I've faced nastier than that! One time, me and my mate ran into a den of trolls—one troll husband and his two wives. He was in the middle of mounting one when I snuck in and sank my teeth right into—"

"Pickles!" Cass clasped a hand to her mouth, though she was smiling and laughing. "Language, please!"

"My first time wasn't as perverted," Anniken said, taking up the lead once more. "I had a full team of four, and we were clearing out a cave. Just the one troll, and it had rooms of pilfered goods, stretching back twenty years! Well excavated and shaped rooms, at that."

"Oh, I envy you! Even if I don't like collecting junk. No, my first time was a simple flush and kill. I picked it off from afar, and then finished it off once it went supine. That one had a pouch of gems, including the prized crimson diamond my contact requested."

"Blood diamond…" That was a very literal interpretation of it, but something similar existed in Meike's world, diamonds mined at the expense of people.

"What about you?" Cass turned her sharp eyes on Meike. "Or was this your first?"

"The latter," they said, cringing. Killing for the sake of killing didn't appeal to Meike, and even trolls deserved some dignity.

Cass waited patiently for Meike to proceed onto the sturdy bridge before taking up her spot at the rear. "Don't worry. There'll be plenty more where that came from. And who knows? We may encounter more in the mine."

Much to Meike's dismay, that troll was not an isolated encounter. Others like it and creatures of equal standing popped up along the road.

Two trolls, possibly the mate of the one they killed, a scrawny wolf, and carnivorous plants guarded the way, and were quickly dispatched of.

Being at the front of the procession, Anniken handled most of the monsters, only abandoning Vallens once to chase down a troll. Otherwise, she gladly allowed her horse to trample everything else underfoot, delivering final blows with swift blows and slashes.

Pickles trotted along, tackling anything she missed, while Cass and Meike provided support from afar. It was rather efficient, and they appreciated being a part of the fray.

"I'm not convinced this road is patrolled at all," Cass said, with a sniff. She'd tucked her bow away in favor of slinging fireballs and bolts of lightning at their enemies. It saved her ammo and hassle, she claimed. "Or that anyone has been by this way in years."

"There are other routes," Anniken said. Her voice was tense, and she kept her back to the group. "The country at the other end of this road is just as much to blame."

"Why is that?" Meike spoke up, mostly to dispel the tension between the two women. It was going to be a long and arduous journey, and they didn't want to be on edge throughout.

"There was a dispute in the past," Cass said, while Anniken remained silent. "Once the Silverstone Mine and Ashfort fell apart, there was little need in maintaining the trade route. We gave the neighboring country silver and iron, and in return they gave us salt."

"...Salt?" That couldn't be all, could it?

"Yes, salt." She sighed and took stock of their surroundings. "It'll be dark soon. Do we want to rest for the night, or push on to Ashfort?"

This side of the bridge was far shadier, lined by trees that intersected above, a familiar scene from their first waking in Glasend. One side gradually grew higher, exposing roots, boulders, and the beginning of a steep hill.

"What about the salt?" As far as Meike was concerned, Ashfort could wait. "And what country is this?"

"Payettek…you really don't know your history or geography, do you?"

Meike offered a nervous laugh. "I'm not a local, remember?"

"Obviously. It all comes down to politics, really, and Payettek has troubles of its own. The town of Earfield has similar issues with the monsters in the area. Naturally, no one wants to take responsibility, as Ashfort lies on contested grounds." She smiled, quiet and carrying an edge of scorn. "A game in which former rulers engaged, but their successors might be willing to play ball."

"Maybe we can help," Meike said, hoping Anniken would weigh in. "If we can cull the monsters and get this area under control, the two countries can make amends and—"

"It's not that simple," Anniken snapped, sheathing her sword. "We have no say in the affairs of royalty. Our job is to clear the mine and town, and hold out for Laken and any knights they bring."

"Yeah, but—"

"Don't. How far do you reckon we are from town?"

Cass fed Jasper a treat. "Another hour or two, depending on haste and further disturbances. I'd rather not risk it. We could retire early, and set off before the sun rears its head. That'll give us time to arrive and assess the situation in town."

It became clear to Meike that they had no teeth in this fight. They shifted in place, bottom sore from all the riding. Maybe they could have a word with Laken. She was a revered knight and in a position to consult the Queen.

"We wanna rest," Pickles said, strolling out of the hilly tangle of branches and vines. "It's not much, but I found a stream nearby. Let's refill our casks and find a place to settle for the night."

"I really think we should push on," Anniken said. "It's dangerous on this road, and I'd feel safer knowing the town's within a stone's throw."

"Do you want to put it to a vote? Cause I think you'd lose, girly."

"So far we've established that there are wolves, trolls, and man-eating plants in the forest. There could be something stronger and nocturnal, just waiting for us to let our guard down."

"I think *you're* scared," Meike said, wincing at the sound of their own voice. Not good. Now they had the fiery eyes of Anniken trained on them, along with Pickles' amused smirk.

"What did you say?" Her voice was so low they almost didn't hear her.

"Meike's calling you a chicken! And if they—"

"*Not now*," Cass said, clapping her hands. "You're outnumbered, three to one. Let's find a place for the horses and tent. We'll sleep in shifts. You can go first, but I'm tired and want to rest, as I suspect Meike does."

"I do," they murmured, grateful that someone else was taking charge, and that it was Cass, the most grounded of them all. "My butt hurts."

"Their butt hurts," she echoed. "Shame we can't make a small fire, otherwise I'd make some tea for all of us." She eyed Anniken at these last few words. "But monsters come running to fire like moths..."

"I may have a spot in mind," Pickles said, leading them off the beaten path, a ruined collection of dirt and faded cobblestones, and into a lush patch of grass. He did so notably away from the hillock and the mysteries it carried.

For that, Meike was relieved. Trolls were a bit like moles, in that they favored burrows and the shade of fallen trees. They'd rather take their chances with the common beasts and ravenous plants.

Pickles led them to an odd circle of scattered logs and bushes. He confirmed it was frequented by travelers, and the last left not too long ago. "It's fresh," he said, lip curled. "We aren't the only ones traversing this road."

"Do you think they'll come back?" Cass asked, peering around the area.

Meike didn't care if three hungry hippos came tearing through the forest. They just wanted to sleep.

"Not this late," Pickles said. "I'm going to scout around for a bit, to make sure it's safe."

"Are you sure? You're going to need to rest as much as the rest of us."

"Don't worry about me, Cass." His tail subtly wagged behind him. "I'll take third or fourth watch if I have to."

"We'll work it out later," she said, waving him off.

They took turns leading the mounts to and from the stream, and Pickles returned as Anniken was tying up her horse for the night. He gave the all clear and burrowed into the hollow of a log, curling up among the bugs and fungi.

Meike sat above him, sipping the mulled wine from Cass' flask. It was strong and sharp, but also fruity and sweet. The alcohol was tolerable in this form, but they happily passed it back.

"How do you feel?" She said, after taking a large gulp and passing it to Anniken.

"It makes my head feel funny." Warm, cozy, rather pleasant.

"You should eat something. Can't have our healer hungover before the main event."

They nibbled on a peach pie, silently craving another sip of wine, and hanging on Cass' every word.

"Let Pickles take fourth watch. He may be small, but he's sturdy. Anniken, as one of our strongest fighters, you should take third. I'll take first, with Jasper's assistance. Meike can go second."

"I think it would be wiser to do it in two's, both to hold the other accountable, and in case trouble does show up."

"That's not practical and you know it."

Meike blinked and Anniken was standing, gesturing animatedly. "—wouldn't understand. When's the last time you took a lover?"

"Never," Cass said, with a snort. "And what business is it of yours?"

Another blink, and she was gone. Only Cass remained, and something warm rested heavily on Meike's lap. Drowsy and on the cusp of sleep, they stroked the orange fur—

—and sat up with a jolt as fingers snapped before their eyes.

Meike leaned back to evade the jabbing tips and almost spilled onto the ground below. "Woah!"

"Easy!" Anniken shook their shoulder. "Come on, you slept through your shift."

"What?" They righted themself, rubbing their eyes. "What time is it?"

"Meike, it's your turn to stand watch," she whispered.

Heavy snoring sounded from somewhere below, near their ankles, but they saw no dog or woman. "Do I have to—*ow*." They rubbed the sore spot on their arm, but hopped up quick when Anniken threatened to pinch them again. "You don't have to be so mean," they hissed.

"I'm not being mean. It's called responsibility. And you aren't holding up your end of it. Now come on." She had her sword sheathed at her side.

Meike stifled another yawn and clutched their grimoire. The staff they left with Butterscotch, but they kept their short sword at hand. It was probably better this way; no one wanted a half-asleep mage shooting fireballs into the air.

"Just because you're upset with Laken doesn't mean you have to take it out on me!" It sounded much cooler in their head, but the point came across well enough.

She pinched them again, harder this time. "You shut your mouth! I just want this to be over with already!" Anniken half-dragged them to the fringes of the camp. "If we hadn't stopped, we'd be there now, a roof above our heads and a warm bed..."

"Doubt it." They shook her off. "Ashfort will still be there in the morning! And if we work hard enough, we can clear the mine by nightfall."

"Nightfall? Mighty ambitious, aren't you?"

"Raids don't usually last longer than thirty minutes or an hour. At least, that's how it works in games..." Meike nursed their fresh wound, wary of another onslaught. But they stood still, despite it. "And it's gonna take longer for Laken to get approval—"

"I know! I'm not worried about that part."

"Then what—"

Anniken mumbled, rubbing the back of her neck.

"What?"

"...I miss her," she said, a little louder. "We still have some unfinished business and I'm mad about them cheating on me, but I'd like to prove I'm just as good on my own."

Meike blinked, floored by the amount of information she just flung their way. "Is this a pride thing?" It was *always* a matter of pride with Anniken, but this was weird, even for her.

"Yes." She'd led them further from the camp, into a thick cluster of trees. "You'll understand once you get there."

Get where? "I would just talk to them, if it were me." So many problems in the world could be solved with a simple conversation.

"I wish it was that simple."

Meike nodded along in silence. This was between her and Laken.

She squeezed the hilt of her sword, and Meike glimpsed cold, hard steel before Anniken embedded it into a tree. That definitely wasn't good for the tree, and probably not the sword, either. "You don't understand a word I'm saying, do you?"

"I...understand that you're angry. But I can't relate."

"To the cheating or relationships?"

Meike picked at a scab on their elbow. "Both? I've never dated."

She frowned, lips pursed to say...what, exactly? But Anniken sighed and shook her head. "Why do I even bother?"

"I'm sorry."

"Don't be." She pulled her sword free and turned back towards camp. "You aren't the one at fault."

6

SILVERSTONE MINE

The trip to Ashfort was relatively uneventful, boring, even. But boring was better than random encounters, and for that, Meike was relieved. Anniken was strangely upbeat, however.

"Perhaps the monsters heard of our exploits and wanted to spare themselves the embarrassment," she shamelessly boasted.

"Could be the group before us cleared them out this far back," Cass said, riding alongside Meike. The road widened out along this way, now that they were closer to their destination.

"Question is, how long ago did they come through? Or perhaps that first troll foolishly claimed ownership of the road, thinking no harm would become of him."

Pickles wiggled free of his saddle and dropped to the ground. He shook his butt in the air, tail flickering. "Enough yapping! Let's assess the damage."

He and Anniken confidently strode into the town. From afar it was small and unassuming, overshadowed by the decaying farmhouses and barns in the fields prior. And now that they saw it up close, dismay tugged at Meike's heartstrings.

To call it devastated was to do it no justice. With its ramshackle buildings washed out by the elements and lack of repair, it was hard to believe this was once a thriving town, home to the hardworking miners who unearthed ore and priceless gems. Meike wasn't entirely sure anyone even *lived* here. The first few buildings in the square lacked proper roofing, and some had no doors at all, only gaping holes or shoddy placeholders in their place.

The hair on Meike's neck prickled, and they silently plead with the others to turn back and leave the town forgotten.

But Anniken cried out in delight and pointed at a retreating figure. "Hey," she called out, loud enough to summon most of the town to them. "We aren't here to hurt you! We just want to help, like the others."

The figure disappeared into one of the better fortified buildings, and Meike became acutely aware of the dozens of eyes watching the small group. It only occurred to them now that the townspeople might be hostile to newcomers.

A young boy exited the building, a teenager trailing behind him. All eyes fixated on the elder of the two, decked out in patchwork armor—an iron breastplate too big on him, ripped leather leggings, a snug helmet, and cloth shoes. The sword stood out the most, if only for its unique design.

The curved blade resembled that of a scimitar, but the hilt was missing in favor of heavy wrapping, and the blade itself was a shade of purple. Gems glimmered close to the makeshift hilt, and it carried signs of heavy wear and tear. It could be turned into something respectable, in the right hands.

"Who comes calling upon the Kingdom of Ashe and Gray," the teen yelled, his cracking voice betraying his foray into puberty.

"Oh, drop the act, kid," Anniken called back. She dismounted with ease, and boldly strode forward, stopping short of his sword's reach. "Where's the leader of this town? We're on official business from the Queen herself, and need to take a quick assessment of the town, along with the mine."

The teen flushed beneath his too small helmet. "Do not come into...our town...making demands, you...you..." He awkwardly dragged the back of his hand across his forehead. "Trollop!"

Anniken smirked and laid a hand on the hilt of her sword. "Or what? You can barely get a word out, *boy*." The smaller boy gasped when she unsheathed her sword, making it *sing*, and brought it to the teen's throat with shocking ease. "What's your name, and where are the adults? *Are* there adults?"

The teen stammered, grip loosening and catching his sword at the last second. "I-I am an adult. I'm a man and it's my duty to look after the little ones and the elderly!"

"Is it just you?" A thin red line marred his ruddy skin.

"Please don't," the little boy said, stepping between them, arms spread.

"Terry, get back!" His eyes widened, but the teen remained stationary.

"Marty isn't the only adult! He's just a sentry!"

Anniken removed the blade from Marty's neck, lowering it to his shoulder. "Marty? I'm Zelamir, the leader of this merry band. Point me in the right direction, or I'll claim your head as a trophy." The front of Marty's pants darkened as Anniken's blade pressed into his cheek.

"Yes ma'am," he squealed, and hurried off, sword swinging precariously in the air.

"You didn't have to go and do all that," Cass hissed when the boys were gone.

"I produced results, Cass." She flicked her sword through the air and placed it back in the sheath. "Boys respect a little danger."

"You made him *piss* himself, Zel."

She tossed her long hair back and grinned. "I'll fucking do it again."

The door to the main building reopened, and a third figure joined the boys. Striding with confidence and a dark scowl was a woman with short gray hair and an equally drab robe. Her hair was slicked back with a thick grease, shining in the sunlight.

"What is this about," she said, lips barely moving.

"Rowlie, she—"

"*Quiet*, both of you." She turned on Marty, hand raised as if to strike, and sighed. "For the love of all that is holy, boy, go change your pants. And take your brother with you."

The boys darted away before she could change her mind.

Cass joined Anniken—no, Zelamir. That wolfish grin could only belong to *Zel*. "Pleasure to meet you—Rowlie, was it?"

Rowlie grunted, looking her up and down. "Rolanda. Are you lot with that boy who came by earlier?"

"No, we're a separate party," Zelamir said, retaking the reins. "Here to clear the mine and liberate the village."

"Liberate, she says!" Rolanda spat at Zelamir's feet. "Too many have tried, men better and bigger than you."

Grinning, she gestured to the group. "That's because they didn't have a reliable team at their side."

Meike didn't speak until the group left Ashfort, their horses stabled and being looked after by the townspeople. "Zel, you were pretty scary back there!"

She glanced at them, canines sharp in her sly grin. "I was just playing the role of heroine, is all. You have to put on a strong front for those types, if you hope to survive."

It was her coping mechanism, and for that they could not judge. If anything, Meike aspired to adapt an alias of their own. Or fall back on their old one, Capsule...or something better, but no one here knew them by that handle. No one (aside from Anniken, perhaps) would suspect that it was both an anime and electronica reference.

"There was a better way of doing that," Cass said, cutting into the reverie. "You didn't have to scare the boy! He's traumatized enough already."

"And I can't change time, Cassandra. Let's focus on the task at hand."

Wild grass and flowers grew to their knees, and beneath Meike peeked faded tracks that led to the ruined building at the bottom of the hill.

"Careful now, Jasper," Cass whispered to her familiar. "I'm afraid you can't come with us." Jasper keened and spread his wings. "No, no. Mines aren't a place for a bird," she said, soothing him. "I need you to act as insurance and keep a watch on the town, understand?"

And then he was off, a flash of green in the clear blue sky.

"You should summon your wolf," Cass said, keeping her eyes on the path before her. "She's better suited for close combat."

Vivica! They'd almost forgotten.

"Do it here, before we're locked in with those monsters," Pickles said.

Meike fetched the figure from their pouch and dashed it onto the ground. A bright flash followed, disorienting them. They may never get used to that.

A subdued Vivica stretched and popped stiffened bones and limbs. The wolf's hindquarters and tail shook in the air as she regarded Meike with curious eyes.

"Hey girl," they said, offering their hand for her to sniff.

Vivica gave it a quick whiff and a lick. Satisfied, she wagged her tail and flashed them a toothy grin.

"I missed you too!" They scratched her behind the ears and gave her a strip of jerky, as a treat. There was no time to stop and play with her now, but Vivica could prove herself in other ways.

"Come on," Anniken called back. "With luck, the monsters will be fast asleep."

But she didn't account for the blockage.

Mounds of stone lined the entrance to Silverstone, along with an overturned cart, worn down by the elements and past battles. It would be a tight fit, especially for Meike, but there was a narrow passage they could squeeze through...

There simply had to be a better way. But this was what the enemy wanted, wasn't it? To force them in one by one, so they could easily pick off the invaders? Meike half-heartedly tugged at the cart, but it didn't so much as budge an inch.

Stuck.

"Tch. Let me handle it." Pickles nosed them aside and slid his paws beneath the cart.

"What can you hope to do?" Anniken kicked the cart. "If I can't move it, you sure as hell can't."

A low growl rose from Pickles' throat. He dug his hind paws into the dirt, and with a great shove, forced the cart into an upright position. "Get out of my way." With a twist, he dropped onto his front paws and slammed his back paws into the cart. Anniken jumped to the side when it tilted in her direction. The cart fumbled downhill, coming to a heavy thud at the base.

"Watch it, dog! You could've killed me!"

"I told you to move." Pickles made quick work of the larger stones, setting them aside and allowing the slippery ones to chase after the cart.

"There has to be a better entrance than this one," Cass said. "But I imagine they're hidden out of sight and heavily guarded...presuming the enemy is smart."

"You give them too much credit." He spat on his paws and shoved at a troublesome rock, a small boulder by all rights. "There, that oughta do it..." Behind Pickles, the maw of Silverstone Mine greeted them.

Meike gulped. It looked awfully dark...

"Who wants to do the honors?" Cass held up her hand, fingers splayed. "Among us, I believe only Pickles can't summon a light."

"I'll do it." As the support, it only made sense for Meike to volunteer. Everyone else needed to devote their attention to fighting.

"Very well, but I propose we take turns." She smiled and closed her eyes. "I work best from afar, after all. I'd also like to see these new spells of yours put to the test."

"Me too. I just need time to warm up."

Their first dungeon! Not from the comfort of a gaming chair and controller, but in the flesh!

The warm touch of Vivica's tongue relaxed Meike's hand, clenched so tight their nails left crescent moons in their palm. "It's okay," they said, smiling. "We're going to be okay."

It was Anniken before, and Anniken still, who made the curious foray into the mine, Pickles quick at her heels.

"At least let me check first..."

"Why wouldn't you do that from the start?"

"I was busy!" The sound of vigorous sniffing followed. "We aren't the only ones here."

"That man, you mean?" The darkness swallowed her whole and amplified her voice. "We'll have to keep an eye out for him, too."

"Hold on," Meike whispered, hand extended. A smiling orb of light drifted above Anniken's head, illuminating the area ahead.

But with Cass before them, and Vivica walking side by side, Meike's back broke out in gooseflesh.

If the hard hitters were at the front, who would protect them?

7

BABY TEETH

"Anniken wait," Meike hissed into the consuming darkness. "Buffs," they said, when the others froze and Anniken's presence shifted towards them.

"Shit, buffs! I almost forgot."

A dim glimmer flashed through the group, starting with Meike's sword and working its way back to front.

Cass whispered a thank you and turned back to their fearless leaders. Meike didn't know what they expected when first stepping into the mine, but it wasn't *this*.

For starters, the tunnel they started in sloped downwards in a spiral. Nothing but rock surrounded them on either side, occasionally growing thin at turns. Meike petted Vivica to soothe their nerves, the one thing between them and the impenetrable darkness behind. Their light wasn't strong enough to cover more than two feet at a time.

And then there was the silence, stifling and utterly devoid of life. There was no banter to be had, no contentious back and forth between Anniken and Pickles, no demands of silence from Cass.

Nothing.

Meike touched the rugged stone wall, their staff carefully tucked under one arm and held aloft to avoid scuffling. The walls offered no story they perceived, only of centuries old excavations, and a hint of the ore it was known for.

They left symbols for themself at each turn, simple markers in the Mythic Script, magical breadcrumbs should they get lost.

Cass stopped, and Meike almost crashed into her, apologies on their lips. She pressed a hand into their side and let out a sharp exhale. She uncurled her fingers one at a time, leaving four extended.

Four. Four enemies or heart beats?

Meike touched her hand in understanding, and she nodded.

And then came the sounds of many small feet and ragged breaths. Pickles growled, and Anniken's sword whistled through the air. A sharp *clang* pierced Meike's ears, but they bit back a groan, almost losing their staff to cover their ears from the harsh sounds of combat.

"Kobolds," Cass said, as the racket died down. "Dreadful things…"

The party paused long enough to allow looting of the bodies—what little there was to take, anyway—fangs, claws, and the odd coin were the only items of note. Meike picked up a tiny dagger, roughly the size of a butter knife. Hard to believe kobolds could survive in the wild with these.

The passage widened into a large room littered with empty nodes, overturned carts, and odd bits of machinery, tracks pried from the tunnels, and a pile of miscellaneous bones. Some too small or big to belong to a human.

"So this is their front parlor," Anniken muttered, kicking the bones. "I think we only killed their sentries. There will be more coming this way or in one of those tunnels." She nodded at one of many passages.

Meike didn't like that one bit. They shrank back, but Vivica tugged on their cloak, urging them forward.

"Pickles, what do you think?"

He lowered his head to the ground, sniffing with urgency. "Mostly kobolds up ahead, but there's the reek of trolls further down. We can save them for last and focus down the little guys first." He wandered closer to the nearest passages, took a quick sniff, and darted back. "I smell that stranger, too. I think he may have cleared several rooms already, but it couldn't hurt to double check."

"Right, him...he's going to be trouble, isn't he?"

"Doubtful. There's just one of him, but four of us." Pickles stretched out, butt wiggling in the air. "I can take on a bunch of oversized lizards. Wanna split up?"

"No!" Meike winced at their voice echoing through the room. "Never split the party! We don't know what we're working with here."

"I don't see the harm," Cass said. "Pickles can handle himself, but we should at least go two and two."

"I told you, I don't need help!" Pickles sauntered off into the tunnel without further word.

"Pickles!"

Anniken motioned for them to be quiet. "Meike, you and Vivica can take the next tunnel over. If there's trouble, call for me or Pickles. Cass and I can pair up."

"...you're leaving me?" Panic swelled in their chest. They trusted Vivica, but what if there were over four kobolds? A dozen or double that? Could a mage in training and their tamed wolf really hold their own?

Cass gave them a reassuring pat on the back. "You'll be fine. Vivica can warn you, and we'll linger for five minutes."

They worried the staff in their hands. "You mean it?"

"Yes! And Pickles is fast. I'm sure he'll have his area cleaned before you're finished. He'll come looking for you."

"Alright," they said, not entirely convinced, but left with little choice in the matter. Trusting was all they could do at the moment.

Vivica boldly trotted into the designated tunnel. She turned and barked for Meike to follow.

It was decided, then.

While Vivica continued ahead, Meike refreshed the Light and sent it forward. Behind them, a similar glow lit the main chamber. Cass' doing, they assumed.

Vivica padded on, heedless of the darkness beyond Meike's Light.

"Do you see anything?"

She let out a low woof and pointed her snout into the depths of the tunnel. Meike ran their hand along the wall. Nothing new here; it was as rough and cool as the others.

Vivica lowered her head, sniffing along the wall and ground. Tail bristling, she growled and bounded off, Meike struggling to keep up.

They drove the butt of their staff into the ground as she pounced—

And Meike's brain went blank. The magic danced at their fingertips, which they redirected through their staff. Just as they practiced...

Growls and grunts sounded several feet away, Vivica's dominant above all. Meike caught fleeting glimpses of her wrestling with a kobold from the fire shining at the tip of their staff.

Several kobolds, no bigger than human toddlers, scrambled towards the wolf, wicked weapons raised and at the ready. One lunged with surprising speed and agility, a curved sword aimed at Vivica's neck.

"Vee! Watch out!"

Kobolds were funny little creatures, but there was nothing remotely cute about their grotesque figures and cruel killing instruments. Hatred colored their hateful, pale eyes.

But Vivica paid them no heed, too intent on her target. She buried her teeth into the current kobold at her feet, shaking it vigorously and dislodging its crude dagger.

Meike channeled their worry and indignation into their staff, and by extension, the forming ball of fire. A concentrated beam spewed forth from their staff, catching all in its path, excluding Vivica, who hopped out of the way just in time.

She flung the kobold into the direct path of the licking flames, and caught between Meike's blast and its own allies, the kobold uttered a blood-curdling scream, body pierced and scorched on either end.

Its fellows were less fortunate, taking on the dampened effect of the blast and falling in a heap of charred remains.

Vivica sniffed and pawed at the bodies. She grinned at Meike, who nodded back in awe. Was this the power of the staff, and perhaps even the grimoire? Or was it more a matter of their own will?

"Good girl." They petted her before inspecting the fallen bodies. There wasn't much to salvage, aside from a few foreign coins and a strange bracelet. Or necklace, rather; it was too big to be anything but for a kobold, too small to be more than a bracelet to Meike.

They held the bracelet in the light and almost dropped it.

Bones. The bracelet, too fine and tightly coiled for Meike's wrist, was made of teeth. Some human, boar, or wolf.

Meike's back prickled as they pocketed the strange item. It was too weird to pass up and might appeal to the odd collector.

They shooed Vivica away when she took a curious bite out of a fried kobold. Animals had little to no stipulation over where their next meal came from, but there were certain behaviors Meike didn't want to encourage. "Come on, let's see where this tunnel takes us."

She whined, but abandoned the body to plod into the dimly lit corridor.

Meike sent their Light further ahead. It came to a stop moments later, where it hung and seemed to wave them over. Vivica wandered to it, sniffing idly at the ground. They took that as a sign that nothing of note remained down this way.

The wolf dug at the ground as Meike picked their way over. The Light lowered to greet them as Meike scanned the wall and floor for what caught Vivica's interest. Bones. The skeletal remains of a human in an old miner's uniform, frayed with time and the workings of tiny kobold claws. They nudged Vivica away with their staff and squatted to inspect the body.

This was entirely beyond their expertise, but the state of deterioration matched Pickles' recollection of Silverstone's decline.

Meike collected a scrap of the uniform, particularly what remained of a name badge. The last three letters were faint, almost impossible to see in the low light, but the name looked like "Kendall".

They pocketed that as well, and ever thankful for gloves, searched the moldering remains. The body, long decayed beyond recognition, carried the faint odor of death, a scent that lingered on this closed off corner of the tunnel. A pickax rested in the corner, near an empty burlap sack that might've carried rations or other tools. They poked around that and found a pebble and a very light coin purse.

Pebble bouncing in hand, Meike whistled for Vivica. This was it, then. They expected...more than a body and a few gritty kobolds. It was almost too easy.

Meike's Light darted into the main chamber, bobbing curiously in the air as it surveyed the entrances to the other tunnels. Vivica watched it with disinterest, instead following her nose to Pickles' path. "Vee?"

She woofed and sat in front of the tunnel, tail gently wagging.

"Huh! You beat me out?" Pickles came trotting out, his tail matching Vivica's tempo. "Where are the other two?"

"Don't know. Wanna come find them?"

Pickles sighed and scratched his ear. "May as well. They might've found something good. Or gotten into trouble."

They squeezed the pebble in their hand. "I hope not."

"Whatcha got there?" He rose on his hind paws and Meike held out the pebble. Pickles neatly plucked it from their hand to run it around his odd paws. "Meike...I think this is gold."

"Gold! How can you be sure?"

"I know gold when I see it!" He pressed the pebble back into their hands. "I'm not gonna ask where you found it, but hold onto that."

They added it to their coin purse, and, remembering the strange bracelet, thrust it under his nose. "I also found this."

Pickles eagerly sniffed the bones, curling his lip when he saw the teeth. "Throw that shit away."

"But it might be useful! Or profitable."

"Only a weirdo would want to buy a bunch of discarded bones." He danced around their ankles. "Come on, let's go find the others. We aren't the only ones here, remember?"

Right. The stranger.

8

ANNIE ARE YOU OKAY?

"How far are you willing to take this?"

The plan was to scope out the nearby tunnels for any signs of life or traces of the stranger's trajectory. Anniken hated nothing more than waiting around. She prided herself on being proactive, squishing bugs and problems before they had time to proliferate.

Most of these tunnels led nowhere, the nodes completely dry. She and Cass pocketed tiny nuggets of gold and silver, but encountered neither hoard nor monster.

Had he, this mysterious stranger, truly cleared them all out, or were they hiding in the heart of the mine?

They could explore the mine from top to bottom, but a map would make the process swifter. Her one regret was not demanding one from the villagers (if one did indeed exist), but even the best map wouldn't reveal hidden caches.

This last tunnel just kept going and going, tracing a winding path that gradually sloped downwards, opening into a wider passage, and beyond that, a stairwell.

A thrill rippled down Anniken's spine as cool air caressed her cheeks.

"Zelamir, we've gone far enough as it is." Cass again, and cautious as ever. "Let's go back to the others."

"Right. We need the dog's nose and ears."

"And his eyes." Cass turned back, that Light of hers receding at the very end of the corridor, where the rest of the party patiently waited.

"There you are!" Meike's voice echoed in the chamber. "Oops…"

"Meike, please be quiet," Anniken hissed, massaging her temple. "Don't want to completely give ourselves away."

"I'm afraid it's far too late for that," Cass said. "We made enough of a racket with that first group."

Heeding Anniken's command, Meike whispered, "Did you find more kobolds?"

"Better than kobolds," she said, all smiles now.

"Trolls?"

Cass stepped between them. "We found a way down. What's more, there's a source of fresh air. We may come on the other side of the mountain and discover a monster made exit." She lowered her eyes, meeting Pickles'. "We need your help."

"Leave it to me!" But Pickles deferred to Anniken, who was more than happy to lead the crew deeper into the mines, in that strange passage.

"Let me handle the Light," she said, letting Pickles run ahead. "I need you two to replenish and save your mana stores for the upcoming fight ahead."

Cass nodded, resolute. Meike just looked confused. Nothing new there.

It wasn't the perfect setup by any means; Anniken dearly missed their old questing party, with Casey, Sal, Neun the Shieldmaster, and the sassy healer who threatened to leash troublesome DPSers. *'No, not DPS. Fighters,'* she was quick to remind herself. Leave the flights of fantasy to Meike.

And try as he might, Pickles could never be a true tank; he was too compact to reliably draw aggro...or so she assumed. Meike would know, but Anniken had to see it for herself. Just what was the dog capable of?

"Zelamir?"

"Sorry, I was...recalibrating." With her light to guide the way for human eyes, Anniken stepped into that cool stairwell.

Pickles was further ahead, head low to the ground. Meike's wolf joined in on the action, brushing against Anniken's legs and into the darkness.

"Vee," Meike softly called after her. But it was no use. Corgi and wolf worked in tandem, communicating with a series of yips and barks.

"Do you know what she's saying?"

Meike shook their head. "I don't have that skill yet."

Yet. It wouldn't hurt to learn it for her own sake. If non-mages could summon Magic Lights, why not study the language of beasts?

"Let's work on that together," she said, feeling oddly serene. They were so close to unearthing the secrets of the mine.

She could almost taste it.

Pickles returned alone. "He's been this way. I smell death, so much death. Mostly kobolds, but trolls too."

"I figured as much. There's nowhere else to go."

"I smelled something else..."

"Oh?"

He licked his chops. "Blood. And a lot of it. He may be gravely injured, if he's not dead already."

Anniken grit her teeth. Dead? No, that surely wasn't the case... "I told you we had nothing to fear, but that man...if we can find him in time, we can treat his injuries and get him to safety."

That was Meike's cue to speak up. "We'll find him! I'll personally patch him up." They seemed confident, despite the initial confusion.

Or perhaps that hapless expression was merely for show. Meike often played the role of lost kitten, but their senses were as sharp as a whip. Or maybe Anniken was to blame for making assumptions based on appearance alone.

Like judging a book by its cover, when in reality, bad books were often masked by gorgeous covers. A man with kind eyes could be the devil in disguise, a stuttering creep a shy person with good intent.

And, in her case, a naturally moody expression mistaken for bitchiness.

She smiled now, a genuine attempt that was more lip than teeth. "Yeah, we all have our strengths."

Cass flashed her an odd look. "Yes, let's go. I think I hear the sounds of a struggle up ahead."

Pickles soared down the steps, moving with miraculous ease and agility. Vivica was, by comparison, far clumsier, taking the steps two or three at a time, and almost tumbling on several occasions.

It was the same for the humans of the party; there wasn't a safety rail in sight, and a steep drop to the unfathomable darkness below.

The sounds of combat increased as the ground rushed up to greet them. By the dim light provided by breaks in the ceiling and Magic Lights, blades and shoddily made shields clashed in the air.

Pickles launched himself over the edge, twisting in the air and brandishing his axe. Not one to be outdone, Anniken joined him. She figured if it was good enough for the dog, it was good for her, too.

Behind her, Meike gasped, but Cass clucked her tongue in distaste. All valid concerns, but it was too late to apologize—a sword missed her head, and if not for the leather helm, would've stolen her ear.

Anniken's hand twitched to grab her head and assess the damage, to see the blood trickling through her fingers...

Instead, she unsheathed her sword and slashed deep into the offending monster's arm.

The troll, shoulders hunched and pale from a life underground, roared and raised its sword high above its head. A blow from that—a giant cleaver larping as a sword—would split her right in half.

Anniken darted to the side, a whoosh of air ruffling her cloak and sending a cascade of grit and tiny pebbles into her cheek and sides.

And yet the blade didn't strike the floor.

It met the flat end of a blade just as magnificent—one wielded by a figure much smaller than it and even the agile fencer. Anniken allowed herself one look at the boy, struggling with all his might to fend off the monster.

One hand wrapped firmly around the hilt of his sword, the other braced on the underside of the blade, holding it steady. He bared his teeth in defiance, the veins in his neck screaming from exertion.

It was Vivica who struck first, digging her teeth into a flap of skin on the troll's back. Pickles danced around his ankles, barking and chopping into the thick, leathery flesh.

Meike cheered—"Go, Teddy!"—and flung a fireball at its head.

Blinded and left to claw at its eyes, the troll twisted its cleaver in the air. And seeing the perfect opening, Anniken thrust her blade into its side, swinging in an arc and spilling its innards onto the ground.

"Yes, go Teddy!" Cass sat on the edge of the staircase, feet idly kicking in the air. "You absolute mad lad, you!"

"Cassandra? Meike?" Teddy ducked a clumsy slap. "P-Pickles!" Boyish laughter joined the snarls, grunts, and barks. "What are you all doing here?"

"I could ask the same of you!"

"You know this kid?" Anniken buried her blade into the troll's abused flesh, exacerbating a wound and coating her arm in black fluid, tinted with yellow bile.

Pickles spat out a chunk of flesh. "We were in a party together."

"I see."

"He always overextended."

"Ahh." Anniken wedged her sword into the troll's knee. With Teddy doing similarly, it careened dangerously in the air. "Sounds like you'd be an excellent candidate for a leash!"

"A leash?"

And then the troll fell, landing with a sickening crash that shook the very ground beneath their feet. Even Cass seemed perturbed, but took her time climbing down.

"I can't believe it was our little Teddy this whole time," she said, clapping him on the shoulder. "Gotta say I'm a little disappointed."

"Disappointed? How can you even say that?" He stomped his foot. "After all I did for you!"

"Calm down, boy." She ruffled his hair, not unkindly. "Now, about those injuries..."

"Injuries?" He glanced down at himself, at the dark stain spreading across his chest. Teddy wore armor equivalent to Meike, which is to say, very little. All cloth.

"Oh, you foolish boy," Anniken said. "Meike!"

Their little healer moved into action, swatting at Teddy to put down his sword and apply pressure to his chest.

"How do you feel?"

"I feel fantastic! Did you see the size of that thing? I...we killed it!"

Meike pressed a strong potion to his mouth, and Teddy guzzled it down like a baby at the bottle. And that's when Anniken stopped caring; the medicine in this world was outstanding, almost better than the modern medicine of her home world.

"How'd you meet this kid," she said to Cass, who was busy looting the body before it dissolved.

"Back in Laeford. He's a brat, but perhaps he's gotten better."

Anniken scanned the room, a mess of collapsed tunnels and long decayed bodies. Teddy cleaned up nicely, as evident by the mushy piles of troll flesh and the small carcasses of kobolds.

"Did you get all of them, Teddy?"

He looked up from his spot on the floor, still cradling his closed wounds. "I don't know. I thought they all ran out to get me, but some may have fled when you all came. It's just troll workers and their kobold dogs left."

"Troll workers?" Meike squatted beside him, hugging their knees. "Why would they be working the mine? I thought it was defunct."

"Who knows? Trolls aren't the smartest cats in the barn...but they do like to collect shiny things."

Anniken nodded. Just like Meike, then. "I want to scope out the rest of the mine. We're here on behalf of the Queen."

"The Queen?" Teddy's voice cracked. "Oh, please let me join you—"

"Anyway, I'm going to check things out. Cass, would you like to join me?"

"Sure, now that I know the boy's taken care of. I'm growing antsy from sitting on the sidelines."

"Ha! I can't guarantee you'll find much of a fight with those ratty old dogs, but it's worth a shot."

Teddy's complaints followed them into a tunnel, echoing throughout the chamber. Anniken silently cursed to herself. The boy was well adept with the blade, but was in dire need of a muzzle. But he looked and sounded young. Perhaps he would get better with time and age...if his recklessness didn't kill him first.

"Is he always like this," she said, once the boy's voice faded. Anniken owed that to the distance and winding path of the tunnel, taking them further into the mines.

"Regretfully so," Cass said, gravely. "I proposed dropping him from the party, after numerous warnings and transgressions. He kept antagonizing entire swarms of monsters and overwhelming the rest of us. Pickles and I can hold our own, but the boy was a liability." She sighed and drew her sword. "Moreso to Meike than us. They're still adjusting to the life of an adventurer, and are reticent in...well, you've seen Vivica."

"Meike's not the killing type, I know. But it's really impressive and brave of them to even come out this far. Most people in our situation would be afraid to leave town—er. Laeford," she said, when Cass frowned. That theory about this being purgatory came to mind.

Anniken tried hard to avoid comparisons to anime, especially that exhausting influx of Isekai shows. The boom came after a "trapped in a video game" series exploded in popularity. And to think she was living in a similar scenario...fewer menus, but the fantasy MMO aesthetic remained. And in those shows, there was always the one overpowered solo player brave enough to explore the world and take on powerful enemies and show their worth.

And there were a slew of people who clung to the safety of non-combat zones, often starter towns. She was almost embarrassed by her own complacency, but at least she snapped out of it.

"Some people live their whole lives without leaving their hometown," Cass said. She ran a light finger along the edge of her blade. "My father was one such person. It was my mother,

Catelyn Firetide, who exposed him to the wonders of the world. Him, a man already in his twenty-six year! He lived and worked on a farm, and died there. Supposedly, he claimed to have seen enough after one weekly excursion."

"Supposedly? Were they unmarried, then?"

Cass smiled, bitter and oddly reminiscent. "My mother took many lovers over the course of her long life. Gender was irrelevant to her, as was the concept of marriage. I grew up among many of her partners, and their partners."

"Peacefully, I hope." Cass' mother reminded her of the one thing she was running from. The solution was growing clearer and clearer, but getting there, accepting it...that was the hard part. Unlike Cass, she grew up in a very traditional and heteronormative family. Anniken was the first to really break that mold, through her unwavering attraction to women.

And people like Laken...Laken, who bore some semblance to her now ex, for there was no hope of returning to normality, was there? Of the mundane and fantastical life on Earth.

Cass, perhaps mistaking Anniken's sudden shift in mood, smiled gently and touched her shoulder. "I was spoiled and revered by all in her company. But that roving group of bandits brought no peace onto the Queen's men and rival fractions along the way. I dare say I have more in common with Pickles', for we were not limited by land."

"You! A bandit?" All those worries melted away, but what would Laken think if she knew her beloved Annie was allied with the daughter of a pirate queen?

She laughed and twirled her sword. "No, those days are long behind me now. I branched off from the family when I was seventeen."

"Do the others know?"

"I hadn't planned on telling anyone. It's not the sort of thing that comes up in polite conversation, and I don't want to live under my mother's shadow."

"Right." She could relate to that, in a sense. "And your mother...how did her..." Anniken lowered her voice, as though fearing eavesdroppers—though really, why should she fear? Other than Pickles, the others telegraphed their movements perfectly—and took a gamble, "Polyamorous lifestyle affect you?"

She stared back for a moment, so calmly that Anniken regretted mentioning it at all, and then she broke out in soft, gasping laughter. "I knew from a young age that I wanted nothing to do with relationships, platonic or otherwise! Too much drama and energy than I care to expend. Too many obligations..." She sighed and shook her head. "Come, we've wasted enough time on this already! Let us focus on the task at hand."

Right, the kobolds...there were bound to be more trolls up ahead. Even now, she felt the ground beneath her feet churning from the weight of several bodies, some grander than her own. It kicked up bits of dust and pebbles, though it was difficult to say whether the creatures were moving towards or away from them.

And then there was the matter of the smell! The reek of hundreds of unwashed bodies and waste. It was enough to make anyone gag, and Anniken fought it as well as any other. She had to.

Cass flashed her blade in the dim glow of her summoned Light. "Do me a kindness and mention my past to no one, Zelamir."

"Of course," she whispered, tiptoeing down the stairs onto the final landing, for how deep could the mines go? And the commotion at their feet, no, all around them, rose with striking foreboding and clarity, bringing with it the minute grunts of tiny beings hard at work, and the strident yells of their handlers.

Anniken held up a hand and slowly extended her fingers. Cass placed a steady hand on her shoulder in acknowledgment. This was a job better suited for someone of Pickles' build and swiftness, but Anniken played the role now, creeping away from the safety of the staircase, to the system of corridors, cordoned off by flimsy strips of cloth and leather.

And between the gaps she spied them—the small, frail bodies of kobolds, dressed in little more than loincloths, hammering away at iron and silver nodes. And wandering the rows with whip and lash, were the grotesque trolls, smaller and lithe, unlike the fallen guardsman above.

She stifled a cough and made her way back to Cass, just as a kobold went flying from the lash. This wasn't a job for one person, and that fool Teddy would get himself killed if he went in thinking so. This was barely a job for their ragtag group of Adventurers, but she had to prove herself.

To Laken, to Queen Illora, but most importantly, herself.

9

OUR LIPS ARE SEALED

"**Y**ou should count your hides lucky they didn't see you!"

Anniken and Cass couldn't have been gone longer than twenty minutes, and in that time Meike's anxiety was slowly climbing off the charts.

Not only did they have Teddy to worry about (who they were genuinely happy to see), but also any potential monsters lurking about. And honestly, given Teddy's track record, it was hard to say which was worse.

They kept a firm hand on Teddy's shoulder, who was blocked on the other side by Vivica. She had one end of his cape neatly tucked into her mouth, ready to gag him at any moment.

Teddy was squirming and gently pleading with Vivica to ease off when Anniken appeared, paler than usual and breathing heavily. She looked unnerved but oddly determined.

"And just where did you two go off to?" Pickles trotted towards her, teeth bared.

Uh oh...

"We've got trouble up ahead. Teddy—" She looked at him now, but Pickles let out a sharp bark.

"Is a child. I'd expect the little twerp to go off half-cocked, but I thought you were smarter than that." His lip curled in a sneer. "How bad is it?"

Cass stepped around Anniken, sparing her a quick glance. "One troll to twenty kobolds, by my estimate. It's got the kobolds at work."

"They didn't see you, did they?"

"No, I don't believe so. We left after assessing the situation, but it's obvious this isn't a task for one person." Her eyes darted to Teddy, who bowed his head in resignation. "I worry if the six of us will even be enough. We'd need a plan, at the very least."

"I have a question for you, Pickles." Anniken, who'd taken the backseat to allow Cass the floor, side eyed the corgi.

"Shoot."

"Why didn't you recognize Teddy's scent earlier? Are your senses working properly?"

That was a question Meike had of their own, once the dust settled. They'd traveled together long enough for Pickles to memorize Teddy's scent. Either his nose was broken, or he wasn't very observant.

Pickles growled. "I can't detect what isn't there. Now stop changing the fucking subject. Cass, what do you propose?"

"We swoop in and hit them hard. I noted several fire hazards, so Meike, you and I are going to light them up. Pickles, you and Zelamir can rush in and clean house!"

"What about me," Teddy piped up. "I can clear a room on my—" He made a dreadful retching sound as Vivica tugged on his cape.

"I want Pickles to lead the fray, as he's our heavy hitter, and nimble enough to scout ahead. Teddy..." She pointed at him. "I want you to hang back and focus on the kobolds. Meike, you control Vee as you see fit, but I want you to switch to support afterwards, understand?"

Meike felt a swell of pride on Vivica's behalf, and more for their own role in this. They were still new to the role of tactician; back in the Old World, they relied on the tanks and healers to instruct the team. But they had the chance now to turn it all around, to make their mark, to be the one who got to call the shots! Cass clearly had practice with it, which they attributed to her age and relation to this world.

"Understood!" They gave a sharp salute.

"Pickles, the path is straightforward, and you won't be able to miss it, for the smell."

"Yeah, yeah. I already know what to expect from that lot." He darted forward, scrambling on all fours.

Meike leaned on Teddy on the descent; the staircase was rubbed smooth in some places, and the steep decline almost sent them tumbling several times.

"It's okay," Teddy whispered, smiling at them over his shoulder. "I've got you covered."

"Thanks, Ted." But Meike felt confident in their little band. After the demonstration above, they believed the worse was behind them now. That troll was the worst of things to come.

That was until the reek hit them like a strike across the face. Meike coughed into their poncho, gagging on the rancid smell of filth. But there was no time to adjust, for Pickles let out a loud, sharp bark, and Cass yelled, "Now!"

Fire lit the room, dazzling Meike, who hastily shielded their eyes against the ensuing flames and smoke. The clashing of swords and high-pitched wails assailed their ears, and the once foul smell deviated into burning flesh and hair. It was utter chaos, and overwhelmed and horrified at what they might see, Meike buried their head into their cloak and stood back against a wall.

Teddy and Vivica left their side to join the fray. There was snarling now, from all ends and sources. Vivica yelped, but the kobold she wrestled with screamed louder. It struck the wall with a solid thud, and the ground beneath their feet pattered with the slapping of feet and thudding of bodies.

Anniken laughed wildly as a troll groaned in pain, and Pickles barked fervently at something in the distance. And then a hand snagged Meike's shoulder, gently shaking them. "Meike! Get out of the way, lest you be crushed!"

"What—what's happening?" They pulled the cloak down a fraction to peer at the surrounding scene. There was Cass directly before them, her face streaked with soot and a strange, greenish liquid. Teddy flailed wildly behind her and pounced on something with a bundle of loose fabric. He rolled it around his feet, kicking and stomping on it.

"The first wave is over!" She wiped her face with a grimace. "Pickles and Zelamir have gone on already, but I lost track of your wolf. I think she chased after a kobold."

"Vee!" They dropped the cloak from their face and gripped their staff like a bat. "Let's go!" They grabbed Teddy, who came after delivering one last kick to his victim.

In retrospect, shooting off fireballs in close quarters wasn't the best idea, but at least the smoke was minimal. Still, Meike kept their mouth and nose covered as they plunged into the chamber, past abandoned nodes, pickaxes, and fallen bodies. There were at least forty kobolds strewn about, and maybe two trolls in their midst. Good riddance, honestly. Nothing good came from trolls, but perhaps the kobolds were worth saving. Imagine! A kobold familiar...

Meike dismissed the idea when a kobold charged them, a dagger raised and poised at their thigh. They reflexively kicked it away and lost track of it, but Teddy temporarily disappeared from view. He returned with a sly smirk and slashed into the tattered remnants of a curtain. Two kobolds cowered in a corner. Bags and carts of uncut gems and ore laid around them, ripe for the taking.

"Loot..."

"Leave it for now," Cass commanded. "We need to clear out these rapscallions first."

The main chamber connected to a series of smaller rooms, the first of which were all cleared out. Meike spotted Vivica's bushy tail in a distant tunnel, jumping alongside Pickles. Anniken scrambled after a pair of fleeing kobolds.

"This must be their den," Meike said, nudging some rolls along the wall. "The trolls might be on the other end."

"Over here!" Teddy pointed his sword into a room made larger by a series of small and large claws. The deeper grooves in the wall boasted the strength of a troll, likely the one they slayed above.

Meike stepped into it and let out a low whistle. Rags, moldy tunics, and blankets padded the floor. A pair of leggings hung from the wall like a poster, and beneath it laid a heap of seemingly random objects: diamonds among ripped shoes, skulls, parchment, and mundane rocks. Meike wanted to sort through it all, but like Cass said, divvying up loot would have to come later.

"Ya gotta wonder what a bunch of monsters would even want with treasure like this," Teddy said. "And did you see what the kobolds dug up? Do they have their own currency system we don't know about?"

"Anything's possible. Anniken took a quest from an orc once." Or was that an ogre? Meike left a note for themself in the Mythic Script. Those papers were definitely valuable and may in fact be maps of the mine. Or even the troll's diary.

Meike's only regret was not taking a body count from start to finish. The trolls dissolved fast, leaving fleshy mounds behind. The kobolds, however, shriveled into skeletal husks.

They poked one of the odd bodies now. "We can't just leave them down here, can we?"

Anniken sighed and rested on an upturned chest. Odd bits of blood and gore stained her armor, but more clung to her sword. "If we were just passing through, I'd say yes. But we have to hold the fort until help arrives." She tore a scrap of cloth from a dead kobold and used it to clean the filth off her blade.

"But that's going to take forever," Meike whined, leaning on their staff. And they still wanted to collect their loot!

"With that attitude, sure." She flicked a chunk of meat onto the blood streaked wall behind her.

Meike was glad to have missed out on much of the fighting and bloodshed. Kobolds and trolls may be monsters, but they were sentient creatures who were no worse than humans. Their only crime was attacking travelers and terrorizing villagers.

"It just doesn't seem very practical."

"Sorry Meike, but it has to be done. Silverstone is too valuable to leave abandoned."

She had a point there. "I'd feel better about it if there was an easier way to leave and enter the mine."

Anniken gestured vaguely behind her. Right. Pickles followed a breeze to what he believed to be a hidden exit, taking Teddy with him. If he could find functional tracks and a cart, the process would go by with ease.

"I dug up those papers you mentioned." Cass rounded the corner, a bundle of parchment in her arms. "I'm afraid it's in a language I can't parse, known only to trolls."

"Aw..."

"However..." She held up a rolled piece, in a greater state of deterioration. "I found part of a map to the upper floors. There are a few hidden nooks and crannies I wish to inspect before we leave."

"We really should have someone watch the front entrance," Anniken said, sheathing her sword. "I can go there now, if you two want to poke around. Just send word to the boys first."

Cass clucked her tongue. "No, Zel, *you* stay here. I need to touch base with Jasper." She held up her PDA. "And besides—Pickles doesn't carry one of these, and I'm not so sure about the boy."

"Ugh, I guess I can pair up with Pickles, and Teddy can tag along with Meike."

"Can we at least confirm if he has a PDA or not," Meike said, waving their hands in the air. Why did everyone try to decide for them?

But if she wanted to pair up with Pickles, that was fine by them. The two didn't always get along, but Teddy was unknown to Anniken. At least with Pickles, there was some familiarity and not so playful ribbing. But Teddy...

Needed a leash.

Meike fell a step behind Anniken, allowing her to lead the way through the winding tunnels. During the descent, Meike ignored the closed in feeling of the surrounding walls by focusing on the task at hand, of intercepting the trolls and their minions. That mix of fear and adrenaline kept the quiet terror at bay.

The tightness of the passages, the lack of a fresh breeze, the musty smell of death and decay...

They suddenly felt the need to get out, to flee like a trapped rabbit in its burrow. If they had to claw and bite their way out, so be it. But Vivica licked their hand and uttered a soft whine of concern. She sat on her haunches, head tilted and wise eyes boring into theirs.

Meike eased their grip on their staff and blinked at the paleness of their knuckles. The room they'd found themself in was dimly lit not by magic, but by a cluster of mushrooms growing along one side of the wall. Pale blue mushrooms...

They carefully traced their pinky finger along one. It had the consistency of jello and hummed gently at their touch. "Cool," they murmured. Maybe they could take one home as a souvenir.

Or...maybe not. What if it failed to thrive outside this environment? What if it was secret magic or tech created by the trolls? Might be safer to construct something similar. With Moira's help, anything was possible.

The sound of Anniken's voice broke their trance, snapping them back to the reality of their current station. This wasn't a simple excavation.

"You do have one of these, don't you?" Anniken held her PDA between index finger and thumb. "Cass went topside to stand guard and sent us back to work out positions. I proposed working with Pickles, since we're familiar with each other."

Teddy flashed his small device with more bells and whistles—a more advanced version of Anniken's PDA. "Of course! What kind of man do you take me for?"

She let out a low whistle. "Nice piece of tech you've got there!"

"Heh. Thank you kindly, milady." He smirked and tucked the device away. "Now, what exactly would you have us do?"

"First—" She pointed at Pickles. "Did you find the exit?"

He sat back on his heels, arms crossed. "We found *a* exit. Looks troll made. I was going to see where it went before you called us back."

"Super! We can check it out together. Meike, Teddy...I want you two to get started on body clean up."

Teddy groaned and complained, but Meike jammed their elbow into his gut. He shot them a bewildered look, but clutched his belly in silence.

"I think we should go by floor. Round up all the bodies and leave them in the biggest chamber. And load them up in carts, if we find any..."

"We found several. I wanted to send the boy down one to see where he'd end up, but again..." Pickles nodded at Anniken. "And be sure to gather what loot you can. We can divide it up later."

Meike shivered. Killing was hard enough, but to sort through dozens of little bodies was almost more than they could stand. But they wanted loot more than anything. That was their little reward from embarking on this journey.

"I hate cleaning," Teddy grumbled, rubbing his sore spot. Meike almost felt bad. Almost.

They turned and nodded resolutely at Vivica, who flashed her teeth in agreement. Meike leaned their staff against the wall and adjusted their gloves.

"Let's do this!"

10

LOOT, GLORIOUS LOOT!

"Eighty-six, eighty-seven, eighty-eight!" Teddy stood triumphantly, one fist pumped into the air.

Meike kept a tally along the way, marking the wall with the Mythic Script. Eighty-eight kobolds and a handful of trolls. The trolls all disintegrated by now, but the kobolds were slow to do so, despite their tiny bodies. Only a few looked particularly "mushy". The others kept the same skeletal appearance.

One by one, they'd piled the bodies into a large chamber. Meike was grateful Pickles found a few carts out back, and happier still when Anniken confirmed a few working tracks. That was how they moved the bodies from the deepest depths of the mine and out into a neighboring field. Meike would've resisted if they had to carry the bodies up the winding staircase. They got winded just going down! And going up empty-handed was a hassle by itself.

Mentally and physically fatigued, Meike sank onto a makeshift cushion—a mix of bedding and clothes found in one of the vacated rooms.

Each kobold had their own storage container of sorts. A few had proper chests, while the rest made do with boxes or stuffed their meager possessions into their bedrolls or pillows. Kobolds were real trash collectors. Meike recoiled several times at the discovery of old bones, teeth, bits of fur, skulls, pebbles, and other trash. Nothing worth keeping or selling, but they left the items in the loot pile.

The trolls had the good stuff—mounds of gems, ores, swords (broken and whole), armor, potions!!—along with the storage of cleaned stones. Teddy may have been spot on about the monsters having their own currency system, but no one could read the records left in scrawling text. Their only option was to ask around for someone who could translate them, or maybe...

Meike sighed and tapped at their AC. Anniken and Teddy had the better devices. The most Meike could do right now was check their virtual pet, status of current quests, and send brief messages to those in range. What they needed was a search engine. But maybe...if they had the skill to communicate with monsters, they could corner a troll and force it to transcribe. Or ask nicely. Intimidation was more Anniken's style. She and Pickles weren't so inclined to ask.

"Hey, what's up?" Teddy squatted beside them, hands resting on his knees. He had a smudge on his nose, whether from blood or dirt, they couldn't say. But it was enough for Meike to inch away.

"I was thinking about what you said about the currency system...would it just be uncut gems and ore, or do they have a way of cutting them?" Or access to a blacksmith who could refine ores and maybe form coins.

"Maybe, but I wouldn't worry about it now. All I know is that even mundane animals exchange favors or share food. Nothing as fancy as this, but..." Teddy shook his head and rose to his feet. "I just got in touch with Zel. She said it's getting dark out and that we should settle in for the night."

Zel. "Did she ask you to call her that?"

"Yeah? It's her name, isn't it?"

"Never mind." Meike patted their rumbling stomach. Loot could wait. They needed a warm meal and a well-deserved rest.

Slowly, the others funneled into the chamber on the first floor. Anniken and Pickles looked tired, but proud. Cass, her bird perched on her shoulder, just looked tired. "I can't wait to be back in the city," she said, leaning against a wall. "Meike, what's for dinner?"

"You're asking *me*?"

"Yeah, Meike," Anniken chipped in, smirking. "Teddy told me you were browsing recipes on your little counter."

"I was not!" They glared at him, but Teddy feigned interest in his boots. "Don't we still have rations? And doesn't Teddy?"

He smiled sheepishly through his messy black hair. "I've got some jerky and a pouch of nuts, so don't worry about me."

"Forget the food," Pickles said. "How are we going to secure the exits?"

Meike saw an opening and jumped on it. "I wondered about that too. The mine is huge, and there's only a few of us. And what if there are secret exits we don't know about?"

Anniken and Pickles exchanged a glance, but it was Cass who spoke next. "So we close off what we can, and station ourselves near the main entrance. We've taken care of the bodies, and the loot has been moved up here, yes?"

"So we just sleep in shifts, like normal?"

"Like normal," she echoed. "I do suggest we have three people stand guard at a time, for half the night. One at the main entrance, another on a lower floor, and a third within the main chamber. I doubt there'll be much trouble early on, so I suggest Meike, Vivica, and Pickles taking the first watch. Anniken, Teddy, and myself can take the last shift. If anything manages to sneak in before our shift, we're bound to notice."

"I'll take up external guard," Pickles said. "Meike, you stick Vivica near a tunnel and take to the lower floor."

"But—"

"If Vivica senses danger, she'll run to you or me. But try to take on what you can."

Meike hugged their knees. Somehow they'd feel safer stumbling around in the dark beneath the open sky. "Fine, but I'm holding you to that!"

"You'll be fine." Anniken gave them a thumbs up. "I'm a light sleeper. Just send me a tell and I'll come running."

"Me too," Teddy said, puffing out his chest. "We'll protect you, Meike!"

"Yes, you big, strong man." She pinched his cheek, and he actually blushed. "Now, how about that dinner?"

The group sat in a rough circle, rations placed in the middle. Teddy threw in his pouch of assorted nuts as an offering. Aside from Meike, who wanted a bit of variety, no one else sampled from the pouch. Instead, they all favored tough jerky and dried fruit. Such was the life of an adventurer. It didn't help that it was cold in the mine, and would only grow colder as the night went on.

Meike longed for a cozy fire and a platter of warm food: thick, savory soup, with fresh baked rolls...their stomach grumbled at the thought, but calmed down as they fed it more nuts and berries. The sooner this quest was done, the better.

Someone passed around a flask of wine, allegedly to provide warmth, and Meike took a few sips for the peace of mind. They knew that some people grew emboldened when drunk, but Meike tried to avoid inebriation. A drunk mage and healer was of no use to anyone, least of all themselves.

"Tell me more about your good friend here," Teddy said. "How do you all know each other?"

"I wouldn't say we're friends," Anniken said, passing the flask to Pickles. "More like...good acquaintances."

Pickles shook the flask and peeked inside. He took a dainty sip and passed it to Meike, who immediately handed it to the next person.

"We met through Meike, naturally. After you left—"

"I was kicked out!"

"When we needed a replacement, Meike recommended her. We work rather well together."

Teddy huffed and plopped a large chunk of jerky into his mouth. "You had rather big shoes to fill, Zelamir, but I see you're more than qualified for the role."

"I can see why you were forced out," Anniken said. She dusted off her hands and leaned against the wall. "I don't plan to be in it for the long haul, so you're more than welcome to take my place. If they'll have you."

"Don't see why they wouldn't. I've matured a lot over the last few weeks."

Cass and Pickles snorted in unison. Jury was still out on that one.

"What do you plan to do after this?" Meike asked, more to stay awake than genuine curiosity. Anniken was the kind of person to pursue a task to the very end, even at her own expense. Whether it was winning back Laken or going on epic quests, she seemed unlikely to set up shop in a small town and hone her tailoring skill.

"What will I do?" She twirled a strand of hair around her finger. "I...haven't actually decided yet."

"Really?"

She shrugged. "Can't act without a plan, kid. And I try not to make plans prematurely."

The conversation lapsed into silence as everyone focused on food and drink. Meike felt a burst of anxiety. If Anniken didn't know, how could they be expected to? True, they had long term goals in mind, but the path to get there was murkier than the future of Ashfort. They were kind of just...winging it until the next best thing came along.

And then Pickles shattered the moment with a crude joke. Most of it went over Meike's head (not that they complained), but it made the others laugh. The break naturally turned to a stimulating recap of Teddy's exploits, but Meike was checked out by then. They politely excused themself from the party and called Vivica to setup at their respective stations.

"I'll head out in a bit," Pickles said, and rejoined talk of trolls and epic battles.

Meike sighed and rubbed their head. Either the wine was getting to them, or they were on the start of an awful headache. "No, Vee," they said when it came to part ways. "You have to stay here."

She whined and tried to follow, but Meike waved her back. Poor thing probably thought she was being abandoned.

They squatted before her and soothed her with pets and gentle words, but she didn't look any happier when they stepped away. "We'll meet up again soon, I promise."

But when she flashed the biggest, wettest puppy dog eyes they'd ever seen, Meike's resolve faltered. They almost considered ignoring instructions and taking her with them, but to do so endangered them all.

Vivica rested her paws on Meike's arm and they rubbed her furry head. "I really wish we shared a common language, but you'll just have to trust me for now, got it?"

She responded with a mournful yap, and slowly walked away, pausing to glance back. When she saw Meike wasn't following, Vivica gave up and plunged deeper into the darkness.

11

I Heard A Rumor

Anniken was no stranger to sleeping in strange and uncomfortable places, from the Black Forest of Germany to Yellowstone. She'd survived treacherous weather and scared off scavenging bears. And bears were objectively scarier than the common troll.

A troll wouldn't drag you out of your tent and devour you alive, ignoring screams and feeble attempts at escape.

So why was she finding it hard to fall asleep, while the others around her drifted off with ease?

Desperate of a little pick me up, Anniken reached for the one thing that gave her hope at times like these: her PDA. She winced at the burst of artificial light, but saw no sign of complaint. Safe.

That fool Teddy was out like a light, but snoring up a storm. He was bound to rouse the nearby town and surrounding forest. It was Pickles' idea for them to pile up like hamsters; safety in numbers, and all that. Teddy slept in Meike's bedroll, a few paces away from the women.

A low hiss in the dark almost made Anniken drop her PDA, but she was relieved to see it was just Cass. "Zelamir," she whispered, stooping beside Teddy's body. "Put that thing away and get some sleep!" She rolled Teddy onto his side, and the snoring abruptly stopped, further aided by the thumb tucked in his mouth.

"I will." She rolled onto her side, curving a protective hand over her PDA. "I just wanted to send a quick message to Laken."

"Can't it wait until morning? Help won't arrive for several days, and texting her in the dead of the night won't expedite that." She lingered by Teddy, but he uttered not a peep. "Teddy's a loose cannon, but you've got some sense. I admire that about you," she added, voice softening near the end.

Anniken's ears warmed, but she gave no response, only focused on the screen before her. Short and professional was the goal here.

Zelamir

Laken, we've cleared the mine. Almost 100 kobolds and less than 10 trolls. We uncovered mounds of treasure and strange letters in the troll tongue. How long do you think it'll take for you to get here? We can't hold it forever.

Content and relieved at the ease of writing the message, Anniken spent twelve minutes agonizing over tone and length before hitting the dreaded send button.

She let out a shaky breath and tucked the device beneath her pillow. Laken...Her Laken. Thoughts of the Knight filtered through her mind. Some pleasant, but mostly tinged with bitterness. It was foolish getting invested in a new relationship that fast.

Filling a void.

She needed a distraction, some semblance of normality in a strange new land. And who better than her knight in shining armor? Tall, strong, handsome, charming...

Anniken retreated beneath her blanket. She focused on the soft breaths of her teammates, relieved to have something new to fixate on, even if it turned into gradual snores from Teddy. *'Steady breaths, empty your mind, relax your body, and just breathe...'*

She repeated that mantra until she too fell into a deep sleep and a soothing dream. A familiar scene from happier times, Anniken leaning back into Laken's strong arms, as they rode on Fallon's back. Anniken held the reins while Laken gently guided the horse with her heels.

Laken wasn't wearing her usual armor today, just some light traveling clothes. This was when Anniken loved her most, though she kept her standard braid. It rested on her shoulder and occasionally brushed against Anniken's cheek.

"You're a natural, Zel. Keep this up, and I'll get you your own mount."

"Can I get a horse like Fallon?"

Fallon, a beautiful horse with fur and mane as white as snow, glanced back with a snort. A snort that said she'd gladly throw her off, if it weren't for Laken.

"Maybe not Fallon...she's a workhorse, built for hard, backbreaking labor and combat."

"You mean heavy armor and running down lesser creatures."

Laken kissed her cheek, a sly hand creeping up Anniken's thigh. She was so warm... "You deserve something light and graceful, sturdy enough for travel and fending off bandits." Nimble fingers tucked into her leggings.

"Laken," she hissed. "You can't!"

"What? No one's around to see. And even if they were, they can't see *this*." She wiggled her fingers and Anniken gripped the reins, horrified. From the tree lines, she thought she saw the curious eyes of villagers peering back at them, giggling and pointing at the display. "It would only be an issue if I touched you up here..."

Fallon gave a warning cry when Anniken dug her heels in.

"Woah, easy now!" Laken took control, steering the horse to the side of the road. "I'll play nice until we reach the inn," she whispered. "And if you're good—"

"Zel. Zel?"

Anniken's stomach painfully contracted at the soft voice teasing her ear. She placed a tentative hand on her chest, where she'd felt Laken's just moments ago. Why did they haunt her, even in her dreams?

"Zelamir!" Not Laken, but Cass. "Please silence that thing. That jingle is driving me up the wall."

The tune to The Adults Are Talking stopped at the press of a button and Cass sighed in relief. To Anniken's horror, she'd only been out for an hour. And Laken responded already?

Laken

I missed you too, baby.

Anniken almost smashed her PDA into a wall. Was she being for real?

Zelamir

Did you get my message or not?

Laken

I did. I was hoping to talk to you right now. We can type or switch to voice?

Anniken worried her lip. Voice calls here were closer to telepathy, but she didn't want to broadcast her thoughts to Laken so soon after her dream. It was...oddly invasive.

Zelamir

I should be resting, actually. I'll be standing watch soon.

Laken

Come on, baby. I won't keep you long.

Laken's husky voice carried perfectly through their words and sent a delicious chill down her spine...

Her face felt hot as she cowered against the wall.

Anniken bit into her pillow to stifle the scream building within. Absolute fuckboi behavior! *Goodnight Laken,* was her final response for the night, but try as she might, Anniken couldn't stay asleep for long.

That damn dream resurfaced again and again, getting increasingly out of hand. She squeezed her thighs together and gently beat her head against her pillow, imagining a thick rock wall beneath her.

Only two hours and forty minutes by her count. And she still had two hours before her shift...

Anniken rolled onto her back with a sigh. It was useless. Five minutes went by, then ten, fifteen, thirty...

'Fuck it.'

If she couldn't sleep, she would turn that energy into something constructive.

A lonely shift of patrol gave Meike plenty of time to craft radical theories. Many crossed their mind during their prolonged silence. One that persisted was so outlandish that it would make them the laughingstock of the party.

But the evidence was there.

The trolls could organize the kobolds and put them to work, mining and refining the ore. They were also literate and potentially had their own monetary system. So with that in mind, were they really any different from humans? Like humans, trolls could be aggressive, but also capable of affection.

And then there were the kobolds. Meike felt a twinge of guilt when they recalled the hiding couple. Or the looted possessions and handcrafted jewelry.

These weren't just mindless monsters.

Meike's sigh turned into a yawn as they placed the odd necklace back in their pocket. No, this was best kept to themself. Moira might appreciate this theory, but this wasn't something they could explain through text.

For now, it was easier to bounce ideas off Vivica, despite the language barrier.

Vivica pressed her damp nose into Meike's hand, softly whining. She looked clean and whole.

"Uneventful night for you too, huh?"

Her ears perked up, detecting a sound unknown to Meike. The soft glow of a light and the head of pale blonde hair immediately put them on high alert.

But Vivica relaxed and bounded towards Anniken, tail gently swaying.

"Zel?" Meike leaned on their staff, adrenaline giving way to exhaustion. "Shouldn't you be resting?" She had roughly twenty minutes before her shift officially started, and she looked an absolute wreck.

Anniken gave a strained smile. "I've rested long enough. Figured I'd get a head start and relieve you now."

"If you're sure..." They patted Vivica, who was starting to whine. "We were going to do one last loop before going topside. And bad stuff always happens to people retiring in movies..."

"Excellent observation, Meike! And I'd hate for anything to happen to you during the transition stage."

"Um...thanks?" Was she feeling okay?

Vivica whined again and wandered off, pausing to peer back at Meike. Whatever was going on with Anniken could wait.

This wasn't the first time Vivica picked up a false lead, but Meike was willing to hear her out, on the off chance there was a legit threat. They kept to the back, allowing Anniken to closely tail the wolf.

"Come on, Vee, we've gone far enough."

She'd led them down one of the winding tunnels, but stopped near the bend. Vivica's ears flattened, and she pulled her lips back in a silent snarl.

Anniken glanced back at them and made a shushing gesture. What did they notice that Meike didn't? "Don't you hear that," she mouthed.

They opened their mouth, paused, and shook their head. It was dead quiet down here, but Meike heard nothing but the faint whistle of wind from a distance. The same all night during their shift.

Vivica stepped forward, head lowered. And that's when they heard it—the shuffling of light feet on stone, along with ragged breathing.

The kobold stumbled around the corner, its face dimly illuminated by the glowing device in its claws. It had enough time to squeak in alarm before Vivica pounced on it.

Meike started to cry out, but the kobold went down without a fight, the device clattering to the ground. Vivica jerked her head sharply to the side and dropped the small body.

"Good girl," Anniken whispered. "Safe to say this one was a scout, but there may be more. Let's go on ahead."

"Now? What about the others?"

"No time!"

Meike groaned. But their shift was almost over! It was like having a customer approach you five minutes before your break...

They stooped to collect the abandoned device. The vermin all collected useless junk, but this was the rare treasure.

A simple AC, nowhere close to a PDA, but perhaps the kobold used it as a pure communications device. There would be plenty of time to inspect it later, when they weren't going along with Anniken's suicide mission.

She moved at a light jog, guided along by an invisible motor. It was too much for Meike, who would never be in peak physical condition and had no desire to be.

"Zel," they wheezed, leaning heavily on their staff. "The others will be up by now. Shouldn't we go back?"

"Not until we get to the bottom of this!"

If that didn't come soon, they'd collapse in the stairwell and wait for her return. She went from looking half-dead to prancing with as much energy as a puppy and showed no signs of slowing down.

"Look!" Anniken shook their arm and nodded at a slit in the wall. And just beyond it...

They gripped her arm in turn. "Trolls!"

Just outside the hole in the wall were the croaking voices of one large creature, and the high-pitched chirps of a smaller one. Were they waiting to hear from the scout?

Meike placed their mouth near Anniken's ear. "What should we do?"

"Go back, unless you want to take them all on?"

All? They didn't know how many there were!

"Regardless, there must not be a lot of them. Come, let's find Cass."

Meike marked the passage with the Mythic Script, leaving smaller breadcrumbs on the way back up.

Why were there monsters here? Did they come to check on the collected ore? Or did the trolls and kobolds work in shifts, sending their colleagues back to ragtag families in dank, cavernous homes?

They giggled to themself at the image of a kobold housewife tending to her pups while the hardworking father toiled away in the mine. The looted AC surely held some clue, but Meike wanted nothing more than to sleep.

Let Anniken and Cass handle recon.

"Well done, Zelamir!"

For some tortuous reason, they forbade Meike from retiring to bed. They remained propped up with their staff, poncho hanging loosely over their eyes. Lucky Teddy was snoozing away while the others stood in a tight circle, talking animatedly amongst themselves.

"If we act now, we can track down their hideouts and maybe the elusive *Goblin Market*."

Cass uttered a throaty chuckle. "Doubtful, Zel! But I'll send Jasper out on a little reconnaissance. It's 'bout time he earned his keep."

"Excellent! I received a timid response from Laken. They'll be rousing their men soon. We just have to survive another night or three."

Meike held back a yawn. *Three* nights? Was she serious? And what was this about a Goblin Market?

The excitable chatter died down to conspiratorial whispers, and by that time Meike had completely checked out. The kobold's AC was tucked in their pocket for safekeeping, or a case of "finder's keeper's," truth be told.

Someone (Anniken or Cass, but certainly not Pickles) came to them after some time, and gently steered Meike towards bed. The bedroll was still warm and smelled vaguely of boy musk, but they were too worn down to care.

Vivica curled up beside them, their staff on the other side.

"Get some rest now, you earned it," she said, despite her mouth remaining firmly shut.

"Sleepy," Meike murmured, and dozed off.

Meike slept like a rock, only rousing when a warm tongue lapped at their face. "Let up, Vee," they groaned, shoving the wolf's snout away. She had a serious case of dog breath, and now Meike was going to reek of it.

"Look who's up," Cass said, waving at them from a corner of the room. Teddy and Pickles were missing, and Anniken was fast asleep in her own bedroll, the blanket pulled over her head.

"Where are the boys?"

"Out scouting the perimeter. It was too risky to go out last night, not without knowing the danger."

Meike's mouth yawned open, the sleep not quite gone from them. Give it a few minutes and a dash of water, and they'd be in tiptop shape. They rubbed the crust and moisture from their eyes. "You said something about Jasper last night..."

"Yes. I had him track down the procession you encountered. Fortunately for us, it appeared to be only a small group. Two trolls, one to drive the cart, and the other to bark orders. I counted three kobolds."

Worry gave way to relief. They could've easily taken on the lot. "But you let them go?"

"For now, aye, but worry not. They sensed something was wrong and retreated. I suspect they'll return in greater numbers, but who knows how long that'll take?"

"I don't want to be here when they come back!"

"Hm, well, better hope Laken pulls through, eh?"

Anxiety steadily creeped into Meike's belly. What if they returned with more trolls, like the behemoth? What then? Giant trolls, riding on the backs of dragons or wyrms.

Cass, seeing the concern on Meike's face, waved them over. "Here, you should eat something." She offered them a small wheel of cheese filled with an array of nuts and seeds. "I had Jasper follow them to their base of operations, where I could safely observe," she said, as Meike nibbled on the cheese. It had a rich, nutty flavor they found agreeable.

"Kinda like scrying?"

"In a way," she said, smiling. "I share a bond with Jasper that allows me to see the world through his eyes."

"Through his eyes," they repeated, fascinated. "And is that something all mages can do?"

"If they know the way, yes. Not everyone can or even cares to, which is a shame." Her lip curled at the word. "It's why I chose a bird as my familiar. They can go far, into places I cannot. You should link with Vivica. I could show you how."

Meike licked a sliver of walnut from their lip. Every day they learned something new, and everyday they grew closer to their dream of being an effective mage. A mage who used their knowledge to help others and forage more efficiently.

Yes, they could sync with Vivica and have her scout out trouble and unexplored areas, but why stop there? Why not harness Saffron's small size and speed to search for mushrooms and ingredients for life saving elixirs?

"I see you're scheming, Meike." She took out a wheel for herself and tore a small piece off. "And I approve. We've got time while waiting for the lads to return, and I've taken the liberty of feeding your wolf for you. Now, call her over."

But Vivica came of her own accord, tongue lolling out. She regarded Meike with curious eyes as they instructed her to sit.

"Maintain eye contact with her and really take in her spirit."

"...What?"

"Oh dear. It's like..." Cass rubbed her mouth. "Nonverbal communication."

"Like telepathy?"

"Sure, let's go with that. Make eye contact and envision yourself conversing with the wolf, of seeing the world from her perspective."

Meike sucked in a breath as they fixed their eyes on Vivica. She stared back, unblinking. What did Vivica dream of when she slept? *Did* she dream?

"I don't think it's working, Cass..."

"You've barely tried! Give it five more minutes."

They stared into the depths of Vivica's golden eyes, but saw only their own reflection staring back at them.

Vivica shifted slightly, a low whine rising from her throat. "Anything?"

"No..." Meike slowly shook their head. "I think I'm missing something."

"Tch. No, I'm just a poor teacher. Although it might help if you could converse with animals..."

"I'll try again later." When they weren't in a monster's former lair... "Still waking up..." Meike tossed Vivica a chunk of cheese. "Actually, did you notice anything off about..." They nodded at Anniken's still body.

"She seemed more uptight than usual, but I chalked it up to her partnership with that knight."

"Laken."

"Aye. Them." She eyed the subtly shifting figure and lowered her voice. "Anniken's in a very vulnerable position right now."

"Yeah, but that's why we're here—*oh*."

"Just try to be understanding and help distract her. It's only going to get worse."

Meike watched Anniken with mounting curiosity. Next to Teddy, they were probably the least qualified in the group to give advice on love. "By the way, I heard y'all saying something about a Goblin Market before I drifted off." Or had they merely imagined it?

"I wondered about that. You were asleep on your feet by the time I got you in bed." Cass chuckled to herself. "And the Goblin Market is an old fairy tale. At least that's how it was presented to me. Strange creatures selling exotic fruit and other goods...many have studied and tried to confirm the intelligence of humanoid monsters. Most have failed, sadly."

They leaned forward, hands resting on their knees. "How much do you know?"

"Nothing more than a book can tell you. The research notes are widely circulated in libraries. It was groundbreaking work when it was first announced."

"I'll have to keep an eye out when I'm back in Laeford." They still needed a library card, after all.

12

COME ON EILEEN

L aken traced a finger over the screen. For someone who coveted knighthood, Darling Annie got rattled so easily.

A warm arm snaked its way around her waist. "Hey, you're supposed to be paying attention to *me*, Lae Lae," the woman whined. Salje, Selma, Shelley, the exact name escaped her. "I'm not spent yet," she whispered.

While "Starts with an S" had pale blonde hair and gray eyes, she was a poor substitute for Anniken. But she was curvy in all the right places and knew how to work her tongue and hands.

They'd scooped her up in the usual bar and brought her back to the barracks. When Laken tired of their dates, there was always a knight or squire willing to fill in.

"Well, I am," they said curtly, and shrugged off the woman's arm. "You're a good lay, but too mouthy for my tastes."

"Lae Lae..."

The usual song and dance followed, pleas for Laken to reconsider, to give in to pleasure, and enjoy the company of highly desirable women, etcetera.

Sometimes the theatrics were accompanied by slaps and curses, but "Maybe Shelley" went quietly, dropping a well-placed sniff and timid glance.

Laken shoved a handful of gold coins into her hand. "Treat yourself to something nice. And feel free to shack up with one of the men. They'd be glad to have you."

"Maybe I will," she snarled. "With a real gentle*man*."

They grunted and locked the door behind her. No, definitely a poor substitute for their Annie.

The parting words barely left a dent in Laken's armor. They'd heard worse, but rinsed out their mouth with spirits and returned to bed, all the same.

While Anniken tossed and turned, Laken fell into an easy slumber and dreamed of lustful sirens and warrior women, fighting one battle after another. Oddly enough, they awoke feeling heavy in the limbs and sluggish of mind, but Laken had much to do that morning.

Anniken—no, *Zelamir*—was counting on them.

"G'morning," their squire greeted them at the door.

"Moin," Laken said, in the fashion of Anniken's strange tongue. They waved her off when she hastened to lace their boots. "I told you, Char. I don't need your help for this."

"But it's m'job, Ser!" Charlotte propped her hands on her hips, looking adorably stern.

Laken laughed and ruffled her hair. "Really, Char. It's enough that you help me with my armor." And polish it, no less! "But if you insist…"

The girl's eyes lit up at the opportunity. She always fussed over them like a young mother or wife, even going as far to scold them for flirting with maidens. "Tis a dangerous game," she'd say, after each conquest. "You're lucky to not be like the others."

"The others" being knights who sired bastards and left the mothers high and dry.

"Have you heard from Lady Anniken, then?" Charlotte was gifted with short, stocky legs, and had to hurry to match Laken's long strides.

"*Lady* Anniken!" They snagged a fresh roll, stuffed with cheese and eggs, from the kitchens. "She'd blush and get right flustered if she heard you call her such!" They bit into the roll, grimacing at the heat but pushing through it.

When dressed like this, Laken had to play the part, even at the expense of their gender. Most people didn't bat an eye at a woman knight, but there was always one insecure twit ready to start shit. Men like Sir Geffen.

"If we hurry now, we can request an audience with the Queen before she attends the Royal Hunt."

"That again," they said around the roll.

The Royal Hunt was a standard affair and less royal and definitely not a true hunt, but Queen Illora liked to put on airs. Her wife, Lady Alys, was far less impressed by the "hunt," but she enjoyed venison well enough.

"You know she'll ask for you."

"Course she does. I'm 'er 'avorite."

"Ser Laken, please don't talk with your mouth full!"

"Forgive me, Father, for I have sinned," they said, and stuffed the last bit of crust into their mouth. "I told her to put it off for now, seeing as Horace has still yet to wrangle the stag."

"*Still*? But we need the stag to kick off the Harvest season!"

"We can delay it by a week," Laken said, licking the crust from their lips and fingers. "Besides, I have something better in mind than stuffy old traditions."

Charlotte glanced at the gathering of knights and squires in the dining hall and back to Laken. "You mean the defunct mine," she whispered.

"Aye. She'll listen to reason once she hears the news."

"If you say so, Ser..."

"Char, I know so." They winked. "I'm her favorite, remember?"

"And that's what worries me," she mumbled, but fell in line. Charlotte was fiercely loyal, her biggest flaw. She carried a short sword on her hip, a mere toy compared to Laken's longsword.

Knight and squire navigated the barracks to a hidden exit that led to the castle, safe from the fawning gaze of Laken's many admirers and the common townsfolk.

"Keep your wits about you, Ser," Charlotte said outside the throne room. "The Queen—"

"Loves me," they said, flagging down one of her ladies-in-waiting. "She'll be like putty in my hands."

Charlotte tightened her grip around Laken's cape. "Ser, please. Remember the cause."

"You worry too much, Char." They offered a light bow to the approaching young woman.

She sniffed and crossed her arms. "Queen Illora is fresh out the bath, so you've caught her at both the best and worst time."

Laken wiggled their eyebrows. "All that cleaning just to get dirty, eh?"

"*Ser,*" Char hissed, tugging on their cape.

"Please behave yourself, Ser Laken," she said and turned to go. "Come along."

"Wait!" Laken offered Charlotte a mischievous wink. "I didn't get your name. To whom may I thank for arranging this meeting?"

"Eileen. And I'm indifferent to flirtations, so don't waste your breath."

She guided them far away from the Throne Room, to private quarters only frequented by the Royal couple and their dutiful servants, including Laken.

Poor Charlotte sucked in a shaky breath as the decor grew increasingly decadent, gold on teak and a plush couch at every corner.

"I can't," the dear girl gasped outside a luxurious tapestry, depicting a stately woman standing beside a unicorn. Just on the other side came the coquettish laughter of young women, punctuated by soft hands patting flesh.

Laken caught themself grinning like a wolf and corrected their expression before Eileen took notice. They gave Charlotte a comforting pat on the back.

"You should stay out here. I'll only be a moment."

"But who will keep you in line?"

"Me," Eileen said, turning abruptly. She poked her head behind the tapestry, no doubt giving the Queen a head's up.

"I'll behave," they mouthed to a quaking Char, bypassing Eileen and stepping into the room—

"Oh my, Ser Laken. Tis rather rude to approach a lady at her most vulnerable."

—into quite the sight.

Laken chuckled and averted their eyes. Behind them, Eileen clucked her tongue in disapproval.

Queen Illora laid on her belly, a towel covering her lower back. Servants dressed in loose transparent silken garb surrounded her, disregarding Laken as they rubbed oil onto the Queen's tawny skin.

One servant spared Laken a glance, her fingers never pausing as she teased Illora's chestnut brown hair with a comb.

"I take full responsibility. Eileen here was kind enough to warn me, but I assumed I was welcomed, all the same."

"Oh, begone with you! All of you!" Illora waved her servants off, but bade Eileen to stay. "At the request of my beloved," she said stiffly.

Eileen bowed and took her place at Illora's side, who was now seated on the couch, resting an ankle on her knee.

"Lady Alys doesn't trust me?" Laken kept their eyes trained on Illora's collarbone, ignoring the temptation that laid just below.

"Ha! More like she doesn't trust *me*. Come. Sit." She placed a delicate hand on the cushion beside her, a hair's breadth away from her bare thigh.

Laken politely coughed and did as instructed, maintaining a respectful distance from the royal flesh. This close, the heady aroma of honeysuckle and peaches threatened to pull them under, but they remembered the frightful girl behind the curtain, and their complicated feelings for a certain fencer.

"You didn't have to come so heavily dressed," Illora pouted, running her fingers along the shoulder of Laken's tunic.

"I have to keep up appearances, your highness. It wouldn't do to have a knight run amok in their small clothes."

"Prudent as ever, but you take the fun out of it! Alas, the hunt will have to do for now."

Laken's tongue traced a steady path across their lower lip. Fresh from the bath and lovingly coated in oil, Illora's skin glistened in the soft lamplight. One could almost mistake the fifty-six-year-old for a woman half her age.

Rumor had it that she'd found the elixir of life, but those close to her knew money and an excellent skin care routine was her secret.

"You beat me to it."

"Pardon?"

"The stag will have to wait, your highness."

Illora's rich brown eyes glowed, but her smile remained as graceful as ever. "And why, darling, is that?"

"There are more pressing matters at hand, my Queen." They dared to place a hand on her thigh. "I mentioned it to Lady Alys in passing, but there is a party attending to the Silverstone Mine."

"Silverstone! That old thing? No, it's been cleaned out ages ago."

Laken tentatively petted her, like one would a cat. "That was the popular opinion for a time, but I have proof that there's more to it than that."

"Well, get on with it!" She brought her foot to the ground and crossed her arms. "Delay the hunt!"

"You're free to start it without me, but I won't be gone for longer than three days. I promised to personally oversee matters, and will take a small group to assist me."

"Set your mind on this, have you?" She twirled a curl around her finger, making a point to avoid eye contact.

"Yes, your highness. The trolls and their servants have been cleared out, and treasures uncovered. I intend to retrieve the lot as a gift for your beloved wife, if you'll allow it."

Illora hummed to herself, fingers nimbly twirling the strand of hair. "I cannot be won over by bribery, my dear knight. It'll take more than that to sway me."

"Your highness," Eileen warned. "Remember, you are a married woman."

"Quiet, damn you! I'm allowed fun, aren't I?"

"Gems. Cut and uncut, but can be made finer still by human hands. Five days is all I ask."

"Five! Why not ask for a lifetime? The hunt can't wait that long, Lae."

"Three, then." Their hand slid higher up her thigh, inching dangerously close to the hidden corners of her towel. "Two, if I leave now and move like the wind!"

Illora cut her eyes to Eileen, who watched in silent fury. "Three will do. No use in running yourself ragged. I want you in good health for the after party." Her eyes twinkled as Eileen audibly groaned. "And bring a friend, if you're so inclined. You're quite popular with the ladies."

There was only one woman they wanted to introduce to the Queen, but Anniken didn't seem like the sort to enjoy the royal festivities.

13

Do Wolves Dream of Electric Sheep?

Sitting around and waiting for reinforcements was, Meike found, excruciatingly tedious.

While they dared not stray beyond the second floor, they'd explored every nook and cranny at their disposal. Vivica padded along to stand guard, keen eyes taking in what they couldn't.

Anniken and Pickles took turns guarding the main entrance, while Teddy and Cass sorted through the loot. Not for dibs; that was the first activity of the day, and Meike had everything they could want from the pile.

Gems and ores were nice, yes, but they zeroed in on the junk—random marbles, shiny pebbles, strange kobold jewelry, and other fun knickknacks. They were quick to claim a small red diamond, a perfect gift for Moira they planned to personally deliver.

Anniken kicked up a small fuss, warning everyone to not get too attached. Without a mule and just their horses, carrying too much would only slow them down. But she conveniently forgot about Butterscotch. And surely the villagers could spare one cart?

"They will redistribute most of this among the citizens of Ashfort," she'd said. "And the rest rightfully belongs in the Queen's domain."

She'd slept well, but still seemed off, all full of nervous energy, and couldn't keep her eyes off her PDA. Meike reasoned she was chatting with Laken, but the obsession with the device was...concerning. She clung to it like a lifeline.

"Come on, Vee. Let's try syncing again." No better time than now.

They made themself comfortable in a tunnel and Vivica sat in front of them.

"I couldn't do this before, because I was still half awake, but..."

Vivica tilted her head and whined.

"Look at me." Meike pointed two fingers at her eyes, then theirs. "I know we can't communicate directly, but I believe there's a way around this. I mean, people from my world can do it through body language and vibes alone. It's how I tamed you."

She yawned and licked her nose, but maintained eye contact.

"Shoot, I don't know if you understand me, but visualize yourself in a forest...feel the grass beneath your paws..."

Meike could see it perfectly on their end, a wild, untamed forest, briar patches lying on the edges of their vision. Rabbits and deer danced through the forest, but the wolf crept, teeth bared and body tensed to spring.

"I can see you right now. Can you see me? I'm walking in the forest, guiding you. Let's look for a river."

Vivica narrowed her eyes and touched her cold nose to Meike's.

"Just a bit longer, girl. Now, do you see the river? Go on, stand by the edge and look into the water. Do you see me standing beside you?"

In Meike's vision, they saw a shadowy figure standing beside a great wolf with gray fur. Before them was a roaring river. The reflections within rippled, but there was little doubt in their mind.

"See? Are you hungry, girl? There's a deer on the other side, just waiting for you."

Vivica's lip curled, and she stirred. The wolf in Meike's vision tensed and leaped over the river, startling the deer away from its watering hole. Meike wanted to look away from the carnage, but to do so would disrupt the ceremony.

They swallowed back the bile building in their throat. The shadowy figure was gone, and Meike's viewpoint shrank and shifted, until they saw only the deer hide and bits of blood on the grass and fur.

Worse yet, they could almost *taste* what they thought to be venison.

'*Be the wolf. Be Vivica. Be...*'

They choked down the deer carcass, despising themself for enjoying the flesh of a slaughtered animal. The wolf's mind pushed back, insisting this was the way, that predators needed to kill.

'It's the circle of life. Someone has to keep the deer population in check.'

But Meike wasn't a wolf! Eating meat wasn't their way of life.

'It's mine. Stand up or lie down.'

Meike left the remains to stick their snout into the rushing water and caught a glimpse of themself.

Not human, but wolf.

They shook their head and licked the drops from their lips. Meike focused on the hazy figure standing beside them and pushed back from the wolf's body. The world around them fell back, until the wolf was clearly visible below.

Meike waved a hand in front of their face. Less shadow, more form. They clenched their hand and released it. Whole.

"Wowza!"

Being a wolf was cool, but they wouldn't want to do it full-time.

The forest view fell away in bits and pieces, then large chunks, leaving only the dimly lit tunnel and the panting wolf nearby.

"Good girl," Meike said, leaning against the wall. Sweat lined their brow. They tossed her a treat and wiped the sweat away. "Let's break for now and try again, this time within the mine. It'll be awhile before I can really put this to the test."

How much of it was even real? It was one thing to imagine yourself from another creature's eyes, but another to actually *be*.

14

PERFECT SYMMETRY

The view from above was endless and rife with opportunity. Far beneath his wings laid a sea of trees, the unkempt foliage obscuring the winding road from view.

He adjusted his eyes, a tad too sharp, and honed in on a chipmunk darting from a tree stump into the open clearing. The rodent glanced around in the curious way of prey, rubbing its paws together before diving for a dropped fig.

Jasper circled above, contemplating swooping in on it. A quick, easy meal, and a welcome change from the usual fish. Or, were there time to entertain the notion, live bait for a greedy catfish.

But no, Jasper was on a mission.

He clicked his beak in discontent as the chipmunk disappeared into a bush. A trigger fired in his brain, one that urged him to focus only on the road below, and the encampment of foul creatures.

Having accompanied Cass on many adventures, Jasper knew a troll when he saw one. Trolls, much like the base inhabitants of that human settlement, were eager to fell birds. Jasper saw it all the time with ducks and those obnoxious geese. But at least humans usually ate what they caught.

Trolls weren't so kind.

He kept out of reach, green plumage blending in with the changing leaves. Soon it would all be golden, and then barren. The air heralded the changing seasons, and with it came the harvests and grand feasts.

Jasper allowed his body to drop several feet, then perched on a branch a safe distance from the camp. This was as far as he dared to go, despite the urging. A few of the scaly dogs carried slings and arrows, and he had no desire to be caught out.

One of the larger trolls leaned on a heavy wooden club, regurgitating a series of utterances. It gestured wildly in the air, back in the direction Jasper came. A second troll, smaller and wearing a set of spectacles, responded in more refined vocalizations.

Bored with the unintelligible ramblings, Jasper scrutinized the camp. Twenty trolls, several kobolds, and awful lizards the size of horses.

Jasper didn't like that one bit, but these were all important clues for his handler. And satiated, she called him home. For Jasper, home was not a place, but a singular person.

He spread his wings and thrust straight into the air.

Cass pulled back with a sigh. She massaged her eyes, as always, and took a moment to gather her thoughts and settle into her body.

Twenty nasty trolls, brutes armed with clubs the size of young trees. She was less concerned about the kobolds, expendable scouts and adequate diggers.

She shivered at the memory of the troll mounts, great slithering reptiles with flickering tongues and salivating jaws...they still had two days worth of travel to cover, but would Laken and her knights arrive in time?

Pickles was stalwart as ever, but the boy was a liability, Meike was timid, and Zelamir lost in turmoil.

A few trolls were no sweat for the team at their best, but twenty well-armed ones, decked out in rugged leather, and assisted by their battle mounts...she didn't like those odds at all, even at full strength.

She glanced at the darkening sky. To make matters worse, it was going to rain. She smelled it on the air, and while she didn't mind a good rainstorm, it would delay Jasper and the knights. What a pain.

The others were scattered among the empty tunnels of their base. Only Pickles kept to the center, curled up on a bundle of rags for a well-earned rest. He rolled over with a yawn, flashing his belly when he spotted her.

"Morning. I have important news for everyone."

He stretched his paws into the air and sighed in contentment. "Told ya. I could smell the stink in the air."

One more good thing for rainstorms: it enhanced a dog's sense of smell. But Pickles was no normal dog.

"Then you know what must be done."

She called for the others to assemble, and they came in various states of alertness. Shockingly, Zelamir was hunched over a tiny screen, white blonde hair obscuring her features. Meike looked refresh and resolute, Vivica at their side. And Teddy...

"What's this about, my fair lady?"

Was being annoying, as always.

Cass ignored him. "We've got trouble. Storms and trolls, mostly. Forget the lower floors and reinforce the main and second floors. We'll have to seal all known exits and prepare for the invasion."

"But what about the people of Ashfort?" It was Meike, of all people, who posed the question.

She hadn't considered the villagers, but they had their own defenses, pitiful as they were. "What about them?"

"Shouldn't we warn them? What if the trolls cut through Ashfort to reach the mine, or target them afterwards?"

"If you feel so strongly about it, why don't you warn them yourself?"

But Meike didn't back down, only nodded. Even Vivica looked determined.

"I'll arm them, too. I'm sure the Queen won't mind if we part with some old equipment. Most of it will have to be smelted down, anyway."

"That's alright with me, but you'll need to request a cart from the village. Your pony is perfect for the task."

"Hey, what about us?" Teddy, the little troublemaker, was itching for some action. And Cass kindly delivered.

"I want you to prepare the weapons for Meike. Lay out at least twenty of the salvageable equips in...alphabetical order, and from smallest to biggest."

He saluted, his boyish face suddenly serious. "Yes, ma'am!"

"Pickles and Anniken—" A demand to put that damn thing down and focus was on the tip of her tongue, but she swallowed it back. "Please begin fortifying the mine. Block off exits and doors to the lowest floors. If you finish that before Meike and Teddy complete their duties, work your way up. This and the second floor are our top priority, and we'll want to make it difficult for intruders."

"Shouldn't I warn Laken? If there are trolls on the road, they'll want to know about it."

"Yes, please. And tell them to hurry. Time is of the essence, and I expect the trolls to be upon us within two days." Possibly even less, which worried her. She tried not to show it, employing her usual mask of aloofness. "I'll get to work up here. Now, go."

15

KID GLOVES

Two thoughts went through Meike's mind when Cass delegated their role: *'She trusts me!'* and *'Cass thinks I'm resourceful!'*

Pride. Pride was the only way to describe the feeling in their chest, and the tiny smirk threatening to overcome their steadfast expression. She didn't treat them as a liability, unlike the flash of disdain she expressed for Teddy.

She saw them more in the light of Anniken or Pickles, not in need of training wheels or close supervision.

"Come on, Vivica!" Meike spared a passing glance at Anniken, who was furiously drafting a message.

Meike didn't understand the complicated relationship between her and Laken, but it couldn't be easy talking to someone you were at odds with. They felt the same about former friends.

Back when times were simpler and slower paced, Meike had the misfortune of interacting with their old friends in MMOs, other online games, and social media. They went from being friendly acquaintances to awkward ex-nobodies, always designated to third wheel status.

Eventually, they found a way to avoid those people altogether, which often meant cutting out mutual friends. But to Meike, it was better to be alone than surrounded by people who made them feel small.

It must be even harder for Anniken, considering Laken's popularity. They didn't envy her one bit.

But Cass—*that* was someone worth emulating! The way she took charge, herding them like a shepherd with their flock...that's how a tactician operated. *That* was Meike's true calling.

'Whoever controls the buffs controls the universe!'

They laughed at their own joke, startling Vivica. Fortunately, no one but the wolf was around to hear it.

Meike blinked as they stepped into the sunlight; being cooped in darkness for two days did that to a person. But no one was happier than a beast accustomed to the great outdoors.

Vivica ran ahead, tail wagging as she savored the fresh air and unruly grass. She dug aimlessly at the dirt. It almost made Meike want to grab their fishing rod and wade into the nearest stream.

They caught up with her and patted her back. "Don't worry, girl. When this is all over, we'll go for a nice, peaceful walk through the meadow. I'll catch you a few fish and forage around for kelp and..." Something. They'd find something.

But right now, they had to make Cass proud!

Meike almost tripped on the way down the hill, but picked themself up and dropped to a casual stroll. No use in riling up the already anxious villagers.

The uncanny feeling of disembodied eyes unnerved them, but Meike put on a brave face—not quite Zelamir's caliber, but enough to inspire confidence. Mostly in themself.

"Hello?"

"Oh," Meike said, taking in the little boy they met days ago. "Terry, right?"

He looked underfed and scrawny beneath his dirty wool tunic, which he wore like a dress. Belted at his side was a wooden dagger.

"Yeah. Where are the rest of you?" He side eyed Vivica, a mix of fear and delight in his eyes.

"In the mine! Can you do me a favor and fetch Rowlie for me? Or your...brother?"

"Marty's not my brother." He pointed behind him without turning. "He's guarding the wall. And Rowlie is taking a nap." Terry tapped his forehead. "She's seeing auras."

"Like a migraine?"

Terry shrugged. "I don't know! I just know she gets upset if I play too loudly." He pressed a finger to his lips. "You have to be real quiet! But I can help. I'm training to be a knight," he said with a level of gravitas that was enviable.

"Are there any other adults I could talk to?"

"No...they're all resting or defending the town. I can help."

Meike sighed and crouched to his level. "Terry, this isn't a game. You're all in grave danger."

"Oh no!" But his tone and expression didn't match the urgency of the situation. "Is it trolls again?"

"Bigger, meaner trolls. And they're angry that we've re-taken the mine."

He raised his eyebrows. "You took back Silverstone? But then why are the trolls coming back?"

"I..." He had a point. "Please go get Marty. We can provide you with weapons in case the trolls target the town."

"But why would they do that? Silverstone has nothing to do with Ashfort."

"Just trust me! This is super important."

The boy hurried off, clinging to his toy dagger. He was scarcely larger than a kobold himself...Meike didn't want to think about him becoming a target for the monsters. A little rag doll with a toy blade.

Terry returned minutes later with the patchwork guard. He wore the same tattered pants, minus the incriminating stain.

Marty glanced over Meike's shoulder and visibly relaxed. "Hello! Terry says you have intel for us?"

Finally, someone they could reason with. Meike started with the good news.

"We successfully cleared out the mine and uncovered the trolls' gem trade. But their partners on the outside are sending reinforcements."

"You did—they did—oh. Oh goddess, save us!" He turned deathly pale, spiraling into a colorful array of curses.

Meike lightly coughed. "I know. It's bad. But the Queen herself is sending knights to fend off and secure the area. We're also providing you and the able villagers with weapons."

"The Queen? I thought she'd forgotten all about us..."

"Well, she hasn't! She's going to revitalize the town and maybe even restore the trade routes. So anyway, I just need to borrow a cart to transport the equipment."

Marty nodded along. "I can do that! I'll have to rouse everyone, too. Oh, my honey coated bodacious goddess!"

"Are you done," they said, after the boy ran through increasingly obscure curses.

"Yes, sorry. I can find you a cart, and I'll rouse our strongest fighters until you return!" He darted away without further word, mismatched armor clinking with each step. It inspired very little in terms of confidence.

Meike retrieved their pony from the dilapidated barn, and was relieved to see that everyone was well-fed and taken care of. They hugged Butterscotch and stroked his head until he stopped fussing.

"It won't be much longer, I promise. We just need to take care of a few things..." But the threat of swarming trolls worried them. More so about their mounts, and less so for themself. The animals were completely defenseless, and Meike doubted the trolls could ride or even tame them. Or if they even cared to...

Butterscotch quieted down as Meike hitched the cart to him. It would be awkward going up, but it couldn't be helped.

"Thanks, Marty. I might have a sword that matches your build."

He nodded, face flushed from running about. Another boy, slightly older, was with him. He had sandy blonde hair, watery gray eyes, and wore all leather garb. Meike just hoped most of the fighters weren't school children.

"I want to come with you," Teddy pleaded upon their return.

He'd been antsy throughout the loading process, but Meike had to give the boy some credit—he hadn't dropped or fumbled a single weapon.

"Shouldn't you stay and help with fortifications? Cass won't be happy if she finds out."

"Bugger to Cass," he grumbled. "I'm tired of her pushing me around! And I want to taste fresh air again. I'm sure *you* know what that's like." He pointed at Vivica, who tilted her head to the side.

"Fine, but you should tell her. Don't want her thinking you ran off on your own again, do you?"

"I never run off. I'm not a child..."

"This isn't a game, Teddy," they said, flinching at the memory of Anniken telling them the same. "Tell her or stay here and move rocks."

He reddened but stomped off, disappearing into a side tunnel.

Meike winked at Vivica and turned back to the task at hand. Twenty-two weapons, much of it rusted or broken, but the threat of tetanus might slow the monsters down. They even found a wooden staff, whole but dull and lifeless to the touch. It made them appreciate their own that much more.

Teddy emerged just as Meike was securing the bundle of weapons in the cart. It wasn't an issue coming up, but someone had to walk alongside to prevent any mishaps.

"She said it was fine and to hurry on back. No detours." He snorted. "We need to seal the main entrance before bed."

"Tonight? Isn't it a little too soon?"

"Not as far as Cass is concerned. Said she wants to be prepared."

Meike embraced the silence that followed. They knew peace would fade the second they stepped into town, and sure enough, a small crowd greeted them at the rundown gate.

"See? Told ya I wasn't foolin'," Marty said, pushing his way through the gaggle of youths.

There were almost as many girls as there were boys, all dressed in their own patchwork armor. But only a handful carried proper weapons. Most carried pokers, knives, and other utensils.

"Where are the adults? You can't be older than me," Teddy said, dismayed.

A girl with a fox-like face sneered and jerked her chin at him. "What's age got to do with it, shorty?"

"*Shorty*? I'll have you know my name is Theodore Pengrass, young lass!"

"More like Theo*bore*."

"Nice burn, kid," he said in a flat tone. "Might want to work on your material."

Meike shot Marty a silent plea for help. They were only a few years older than Teddy, but no better at mediation.

"That's enough out of you, Elspeth! These nice people are doing us a kindness—"

"Oh shut up, Marty. Who put you in charge?"

"M-my big brother left me in charge. He said you're to do as I say until he comes home..."

"Yeah, if he ever comes back," a dirty-faced boy chimed in. A kid behind him snickered, and the others followed suit.

Vivica snarled, and the laughter stopped short, petering into nervous titters as the wolf strode over to Marty.

"Now," he said, voice wavering. "They've been so kind to supply us with weapons. While the adults work on fortifying the town, we must arm ourselves and train to join them."

Teddy clapped him on the shoulder. "Rest assured, they shan't reach you. And if they do..." He dragged a finger along his neck, making a dreadful hissing sound.

"We're hoping it doesn't come to that," Meike said, glaring at Teddy. What was he doing!?

One by one, the kids all came up and claimed a weapon. There was more than enough to go around, but Marty insisted the kids leave a few for the adults to pick through.

Meike would've thought it would be the other way around, but the adults probably had the best equips already.

"I wish we could send a scout to warn you when the trolls arrive, but I think it's best you all prepare and lie low."

"We will! Thanks again for the gear!"

Little Terry waved goodbye, a real copper dagger in his tiny hands.

Meike *really* didn't like the idea of child soldiers, but saw no better alternative. The trolls—and while they dare not say it aloud—and the Queen were to blame.

16

KNOCKERS

"You did well, Meike." Cass didn't smile as she said it, but praise from her was good enough on its own.

"Thanks," they said, beaming. "Couldn't have done it without Teddy!"

The boy exchanged his sullen expression for a shy smile. "We made sure the villagers had enough weapons and armor to survive the onslaught. The rest is up to them."

Meike nodded wordlessly. Now that the easy part was out of the way, dread was creeping in. Waiting would be almost as hard as the actual battle. They just wanted it to all be over and be back in a proper bed...

All exits on the first two floors were sealed up tight, with rocks, carts, and other junk lining the tunnels. As instructed, they saved the main exit for last. Cass stressed the need to lock it up extra tight, as it was wide enough for two trolls to walk side by side.

Similar exits existed on lower floors, but weren't as easily traversed.

Anniken sighed and slumped onto her bedroll. "This better be worth it, Cass."

"Whitey, please," Pickles said, sprawling in her lap. "You cheered your ass off when the stairs collapsed!"

Meike sat by her feet. "How did you manage that?"

"A bit of muscle from Pickles. He...it was like something out of an anime. He used a club—troll made, nice and heavy—and just hammered it against one of the higher rungs. The whole thing collapsed in on itself within minutes!"

"What's an anime?" Cass stood further back, the smirk dying from her lips. "Is that some new genre of book?"

"It's...yes. From the Far East. It's very popular among the youth and adults my age and up."

"Hm, I see. I was never a big reader."

Anniken and Meike exchanged knowing glances. It was wild to discuss this so openly, and to have it readily accepted.

"Fun time will have to be cut short. I consulted with Jasper before sending him off for the night."

"What's the verdict?" Anniken asked, rubbing Pickles' belly.

"They'll be upon us by morning, possibly later tonight."

"No surprise there," she said, paling.

"Have you heard anything from Laken?"

She took out her PDA and stared intently at the screen. "Not much has changed since last time, but they're pushing on, despite the coming storm. She wants to reach Ashfort tonigh t..." Her voice cracked near the end.

Pickles petted her shoulder. "It's gonna be alright. Maybe you could make up with them when this is all over."

"Shut *up* Pickles. And get off me, you dirty mutt." She shoved him away and rolled onto her side.

"I don't see what the big deal is. You care about her, don't you?" He leaned on her side, poking his muzzle into her cheek. "You're checking for her messages right now, like you did all day."

"Look, I don't want to talk about it right now! We should all be resting so we're prepared to face these monsters."

"How can we, when you're hung up on your ex?"

"We're on a break," she mumbled, and buried herself under her blanket.

"Give it a rest, Pickles. She's right, we all need to rest." Cass grabbed him by the scruff of the neck and pulled him back. "However, I insist we sleep in shifts, in case they come earlier than expected. Me, Pickles, and Vivica."

Meike, who had only been half paying attention, sat up in alarm. "Wait, why just Vivica?"

"She and Pickles communicate well enough, and they have sharper ears. I just want to be prepared for any early encounters. Don't worry, it'll only be two hour shifts."

"Good enough for me," Teddy said, claiming an empty roll. "Come on, Meike! Zel's got a head start on us!"

"I don't know..." Was it really okay for two of their strongest fighters to stand guard, when they could be resting?

But Meike curled up in their bedroll. Teddy was already asleep, and Anniken had tucked her PDA away.

They took out their pet themed AC, but without a nearby beacon to connect to, it was virtually useless. And even if they could reach out to Moira, she had none of her own...

Cass stopped on her way into the main chamber. "Worry not. This can't be any worse than when we retook the mine."

They also remembered the troll that almost killed Teddy, but kept quiet. Cass was smiling, however faint. And she seemed weary...

"Ha, she forgets that those were working trolls," Anniken said, rolling around to face them. "These are the real deal."

Meike lied on their back, staring at the vast ceiling. Twenty giant trolls and their ferocious mounts...they really didn't like those odds.

"I'm sure it'll be fine...it has to be." It sounded like she was trying to convince herself more than anyone else.

The trolls didn't arrive with a bang, but with a *click*.

Pickles' ears twitched in his sleep, rousing him from a shameless dream of chasing plump rabbits. He rolled onto his back and stretched his paws into the air. The steady *click click click* set his teeth on edge. Worse yet, no one else seemed to notice—no one but Vivica, who stood at the tunnel entrance, head cocked to the side.

He rolled onto his belly, stretching each limb with a satisfying crack. "You hear that too?"

Vivica whined and fixed her eyes on him. Somewhere behind Pickles, Cass stirred and murmured in her sleep. Light sleeper, that one.

"It's been going on for almost an hour now," she said, in a tongue only known to canines. Vivica's accent was thicker and her dialect more in line with wolves than lesser dogs, but he understood her well enough.

"An hour? Shit, why didn't you say so earlier?" He trotted towards her, lowering his tone to avoid waking Cass. "Time is of the essence, girlie!"

"I thought I was imagining things. And it was so faint, I didn't think it worth mentioning."

"How deep do you reckon?"

She huffed and lowered her eyes. "The lowest of the low. They could be chipping away for days before reaching the higher floors. Especially after that little stunt you pulled."

For a creature of the forest, Vivica sure had a refined air about her, and a sultry tone that set Pickles' tail to wagging.

"Pretty impressive though, dontcha agree?"

Vivica turned her head, but not without giving him a hint of those impressive fangs. "I like your style, dog. But you could benefit from a lady's touch."

"Maybe when this is over…" He wiggled his eyebrows and she chuckled, a low rumble in her throat. Not in your lifetime, that laugh said. "Come on, we should alert the humans."

Humans were cursed with inferior senses, but even they couldn't ignore the impending shuffle of troll flesh on rock. It was faint, but the ground beneath his paws subtly rumbled, hungry to swallow him up.

They came across Meike first. The short human was bouncing a ball of flame from hand to hand.

Vivica ran up to them and let out a brisk bark. "Meike! There's danger afoot! Come, come!"

"Huh? Vee? Pickles?" Meike smiled and patted Vivica's head. "Shouldn't you both be resting? You were up for four hours."

"And we slept for two or three." His sense of time was all jacked up. "We can rest when the trolls and their lackeys are dead."

"Did you hear something?" They directed that question to Vivica, who wasn't gifted with the power of speech. She could only whine, yelp, and plead with those gorgeous golden eyes.

Oh, how he hated to see a she-wolf in pain!

Pickles pulled it together, coughing into a hand-like paw. "Vivica did. I assume the trolls have their diggers hard at work."

"The little ones," she said. "Kobolds are better suited for unearthing weak points."

"She says it sounds like kobolds fucking around down there."

Vivica flattened her ears. "Please watch your tongue around my impressionable master."

"It's okay, girl," an oblivious Meike said, stroking her ears. "They can't get at us up here."

"Oh, I hope you're right..." She snapped at Pickles' paw seconds later, when he dared to reach for her muzzle.

"And how are things up here?"

"Not bad. It's kinda boring, really..."

"Boring is good! Do you want to face them head on?"

"No..." They flexed their hand and flames sprouted from their fingertips. "But I've learned some neat tricks. Not just fire, either!"

"Such as?" He wasn't particularly interested in the details, but talking distracted from the annoying clicking in his ears.

"The spells I picked up from a vendor in Zachick. But this?" Their fingers danced in the air, shifting miniature flames from tip to tip. And with a sudden snap of their fingers, the flames dispersed. An instant snuff out!

Pickles lacked magical inclination and the desire to learn, but he respected mages. They were squishy, but really packed a punch.

Meike tapped the bottom of their staff against the ground and muttered an incantation. From the tip of the staff, a dark ball materialized.

Vivica growled and shrank back as two more balls appeared and hung in the air. They traced lazy circles in the air, like oversized slugs. And then one ball shot through the air, disappearing into the dark corners of the chamber. The others followed and returned just as quickly, circling Meike's head.

They waved a hand, and the balls winked out of existence, one by one. "Voila," they said, with a wink and strange hand signal—pointer and middle fingers extended like a pair of rabbit ears. Humans were...strange creatures.

"It's getting louder, Barkenshire," Vivica said, twining around Meike's ankles like an anxious cat.

"Don't worry baby," he cooed. "I gotchu."

She glared at him, lip curling. "I am *not* your baby. Inform Meike, please!"

Pickles sighed. "Meike, things are getting dicey down below."

A click, crinkle, *pop*, followed by the ragged sounds of larger, clumsier claws. Vivica bristled and pawed at the ground, urging Meike to drop the antics.

"How far?"

"Vee? How far?"

She growled, staring ruefully at her paws. "Two floors down. From different angles. They're trying to pinch us." She tilted her head to the side. "Small things, but I sense something bigger scraping at the rock."

Pickles relayed this all to Meike, whose eyes grew bigger and bigger with each word. "Rouse Cass and call the others over. We're about to have company."

17

ADRIFT IN DARKNESS

The first kobold broke through in the dead of night, according to the timer on Meike's AC. 5:15 AM, and they wouldn't have noticed it, if not for Vivica.

A storm raged outside, clashes of thunder and heavy rain drowning out the minuscule sounds of scraping claws. The timing couldn't have been worse, for what better motivator was there than the promise of shelter?

Vivica just shot off into the dark, while the others listlessly patrolled the tunnels.

"Vee," Meike hissed, chasing after her. "Come back, girl, it's not safe!"

"Leave her," Pickles snarled, rooted in place, ears perked. He stood upright, axe in hand. He'd been in a jovial mood up til now, and like Cass, was in a sour mood. Teddy was a bit skittish, and Anniken...

Meike shrugged the thought off. They were feeling nervous, and rightfully so, but Anniken was almost beside herself with worry. She was in no shape to fight, but that might change when backed into a corner. "Vee?"

Just up ahead, a streak of gray fur sharply turned the corner. Meike hurried at the sounds of snarling and frightened squeaks.

Vivica shook the small creature trapped in her jaws, whipping it around with such ferocity that bones snapped and popped out of joints. Meike cringed at the sight. This wasn't the first time they saw her killing with alarming efficiency, but they hated to consider what damage a wolf could do to a human body.

She delivered the kobold's body with a grin, sitting back on her haunches and tilting her head back for scritches.

"Good girl," they said weakly. "Good girl."

The kobold's head rested at an unnatural angle, limbs heaped uselessly around its body. Wide, pale green eyes stared up at them. Shivering, Meike peeled the kobold's eyelids over its bulbous eyes. It almost appeared to be caught in a peaceful slumber—if you ignored everything else.

Meike stripped it of its weapons and archaic communications device, but left the jewelry alone, particularly a lovingly crafted medallion. Lover? Family? Friend? Either way, it seemed inappropriate to loot sentimental items.

They followed Vivica into the winding tunnel, stopping short of the former staircase. And there it was—a hole in the ground, mere inches away from the caved in stairwell.

Vivica attacked it, digging furiously and dipping her snout into the abyss.

"Vee, stop!" They tried pulling her back, but the wolf's fur was hard to grab hold of, and she was far stronger than Meike could ever hope to be. With a triumphant growl, Vivica threw her head back.

Another kobold went sailing through the air, landing with a sickening crunch.

Meike waved Vivica away and crouched over the hole, steeling themself for the worse. They stuck their head in the hole, squinting to adjust to the sudden darkness. It took a few seconds, but they spotted a faint glow several feet below and in a corner. The shape of a head came into focus—small, like the two dead kobolds behind them.

This kobold appeared to have its back to Meike, and was talking and waving to something outside their range of vision. It shrank away, cowering from something much bigger. A troll?

Ugly grunts followed, and the kobold squealed and jerked across the room. It half dragged itself into a corner, whimpering as a shadow cast over its prone body. Vivica growled and shoved at Meike, her claws scrabbling at the ground.

"Back," they whispered, pushing her aside.

Vivica stepped back, head lowered and eyes focused on the open ground. She wanted so badly to nudge them away and dive into the hole after the hulking monster beneath their feet. But they couldn't let her go. The wolf was strong, but the troll was stronger, armed with deadly strength and claws, and that was before you even considered whatever weapons it carried.

More concerning was how close it was to breaching the main hall and to hitting the party directly.

Meike crawled back, taking care to be quiet. There was no point in further alerting the monsters to the knowing eyes of their opponents. Such an act would only serve to embolden them. They ordered Vivica to stay put, but alert Meike if the kobolds widened the gap while they contacted the others. Thank goodness for IMs!

It was their first time sending out a group message like this; before, they got by just fine with one by one mentions.

Capsule

> We've got trouble, and it's bad!

> Vee killed 2 kobolds that were trying to break in. There's a 3rd below and at least 1 troll.

Zelamir

> Shit, you too?

Cass_On_Fire

> How many, Zel? There's two trolls trying to knock down the main entrance, brave bastards.

TeddyBear16

> all clear over here i think! pickles says its a wash and to help the others

Cass_On_Fire

> Zel?

Zelamir

Sorry. I just kicked one in the face. One troll, and like a dozen kobolds.

The kobolds rushed in first, but they had to come in one or two at a time. I stomped them flat, but the troll is pissed.

It's trying to force its way through now.

Capsule

What should we do? I don't think they know I'm here, but...

Cass_On_Fire

Teddy, send Pickles my way. You go to Anniken. Meike...do you think you can hold them off for now?

Capsule

I think so! There don't seem to be more kobolds. And it'll be awhile before the trolls gets up here...

Cass_On_Fire

Good! Hang in there, everyone! This is only the beginning.

Zelamir

Laken says they're close! In another hour or so.

TeddyBear16

> ohgod i dont think i can wait an hour but will try

Meike felt the same way, but couldn't voice that. Everyone was on edge, and they had no escape route. And even if they did, they were surely surrounded at this point.

They leaned against a wall, staff clutched tight in their hands. If they couldn't kill the troll right away, they could at least slow it down. And Meike had just the spell for the job.

Meike's troll caved in the floor with a triumphant yell, but it still had to climb. They didn't give it time to celebrate or climb the rubble, rapping the end of their staff against the ground, and concentrating on the troll.

Large, thorny vines encircled the troll, squeezing and dragging it back to the second floor. It thrashed wildly, club (and some very unfortunate kobolds) forgotten. The kobolds scrambled for cover, but were flattened by falling rubble and the flailing troll. Meike glanced away from brain matter dribbling from a kobold's skull. Unpleasant, but unavoidable.

They conjured up three dark orbs of void matter and unleashed them on the captured troll. One struck it deep in the gut, forcing a pained groan, another collided with its head, and the third shattered its reaching hand.

Stunned, the troll could do nothing as Meike pelted it with a series of fireballs, mindful of the vines. It wouldn't do to give their captive even a sliver of hope. The vines contracted, digging its thorns into the troll's leathery flesh. It emitted a dull scream, limbs struggling in vain.

For a moment, Meike saw the world through the wolf's eyes, tinged with red and a desire to see the troll ripped asunder.

And then it passed, leaving only the pitiful cries of dying kobolds and their slave master. Vivica nodded sagely, perched a safe distance from the widening crater.

"Woah." Was this how Anniken felt, acting as her alter ego?

Vivica offered an abrupt bark. Shame they couldn't understand her...

Just then, Meike's AC made an impatient pinging sound, normally attributed to the pet mini-game. It did that whenever it needed to be fed, played with, or cleaned up, but they could ignore it for hours before its affection meter depleted and it eventually died.

They were almost inclined to ignore it now, but they'd fed and played with it during their shift.

Zelamir

Meike, we've taken care of things on my end. We're going to help the others now. Do you need help?

Capsule:

My troll is dead, but there could be more...Cass said there were twenty.

With yours? Doubtful. They won't be piling up in one spot, but spread out.

They're determined to dig us out, even if they bring the mine down with them.

Meike's heart jumped in their chest. No! They wouldn't do that, would they? Turn this old mine into a tomb?

But that's suicide! No one wins that way...

Maybe that's the point. Come on. We can't do this without you.

They started to argue against that; Meike was no great mediator or tactician, like Cass. They certainly didn't possess Anniken's tenaciousness, Pickles' bravado, or Teddy's fearlessness.

Meike was just a wannabe mage, staying afloat as best they could.

But there was no time to work it out. Zelamir was right. Everyone was counting on them. And hadn't they made it this far? Something in Vivica's golden eyes insisted that, yes, they were brave in their own way. They'd taken down a troll on their own, after all.

Coming!

They pocketed the AC and spared one last glance at the fallen troll and its allies. All dead, or beating on death's door. Meike turned and kicked off, Vivica hot on their heels. The tunnel before them stretched endlessly, the faint light at the end dancing just out of reach.

The sounds of combat touched their ears before Meike broke free and skidded around the corner, staff clenched tightly in their aching hands.

Pickles' reddish tail swished low to the ground as he braced his forepaws against the wall, pushing back against an invisible foe. Teddy leaned beside him, the cords in his neck standing out as he asserted all his strength against the trolls. He would've been better off standing by, but his effort was valiant.

Cass stood several feet away, chanting to herself while Zelamir rested a foot on the wall, knee nearly driven into her chest. "They're determined to get in," she said, spotting them. "We can only hold them off for so long."

"What should I do?" But even as they said it, Meike knew. It worked once, it should work again...or so they hoped.

"Make it quick, whatever it is," Pickles said, lips barely moving from the strain.

This worked best when they could see their prey, but Meike would just have to wing it for now. They closed their eyes and envisioned the exterior of the mines, the sloping hill, and the silhouette of the town just below. A mound of rubble just beyond Pickles' small figure, and two hulking trolls and great reptilian mounts lurking on the other side.

They pictured the thorny vines rising from the ground to embrace the monsters, just like the carnivorous plant once ensnared Meike. The vines snaked around the trolls, binding their arms and legs to their bodies, forcing their heads to the side or against their chest, and rapidly dragging them back and to the hard, craggy ground.

Pickles yelped and staggered forward as the trolls gave up the fight. He glanced around, jaw slack, from the toppled Teddy to the blinking Zelamir, and finally, at Meike.

"I don't know what you just did, kid, but I hope you bought us some time."

"I tried something," they said, suddenly feeling very tired. This magic was perhaps too potent, but it just might get them out of this alive.

18

FOR YOU I WILL

"Ser, I think we should break," Charlotte cried over the raging wind and rain. The poor girl was drenched through and through, swaying on the back of her chestnut colored pony.

Laken continued on, pretending not to hear her over the storm. Their fellow knights, youngsters untested in true battle, and the best they could do on such short notice, followed in grim silence. Even the loudest of complainers gave up after the third hour of being caught in the elements.

They requested a group of seasoned knights, but no, Queen Illora demanded they stay back to help with preparations. For the *Royal Hunt*. Laken noticed their smirking rival before setting out, but paid him no mind. Because Laken had at least one skilled knight in their group, the equally flirtatious Minogue, a fair young man with long, wavy blonde hair.

The difference between them and Minogue was that he favored men—older, hairy, and burly. Zero competition all around.

The handsome Minogue was currently reduced to the status of a drowned, harassed rat, his mouth an austere line on his otherwise gentle face.

He rode up to them now, his magnificent stallion indecipherable from its surroundings. "Laken," he said, in a silken voice too soft for the tumultuous weather, but clear as day, despite that. "I know you're anxious, but the men are discouraged. We need to stop and make camp."

"No."

"We barely had time to rest," he hissed, driving his horse in front of theirs. "Surely two hours won't hurt? At least to see if the storm quiets down."

"*No.*" Two hours? Zelamir could be dead by then. Her last message was calm, but betrayed her fear. They had no doubt she could hold her own until help arrived, but...

"Char," they barked, ignoring Minogue's fierce gaze. "How much further?"

"An hour, maybe half, if we push. But I fear we won't be at full strength without a proper rest."

All this fuss over a little rain? Laken faced worse throughout her career, and more so as a squire. "Anyone who wants to rest is more than welcome to," they called out. "But take heed of the trolls and their battle beasts in the area." The cheers and grins died down. "If you feel comfortable with that risk, then stay. But I'll ride on, with or without you."

Minogue bowed his head, resigned. "I shall accompany you. But I expect you to make up for it later."

"I thought you didn't like women, Minnie," they teased.

"I see no woman before me," he clapped back, grinning broadly. "Now go, before I change my mind!"

Charlotte's estimate was twenty minutes off, but Laken and a few determined knights made it.

"Tch, what foul creatures," Minogue said, lopping off a troll's arm.

He'd caught it by surprise. The damn thing was slacking off by the side of the road, seemingly bathing in the rain, mouth yawned open to collect water. Minogue artfully removed the troll's other arm.

Armless and enraged, the troll awkwardly rolled onto his feet and stumbled towards the knight. Minogue drove his sword into the troll's heart, not flinching as it embraced the blade and rushed for him, mouth yawning open. Teeth grated against the knight's armor, leaving scarcely a scratch in his death throes.

"And that," he said, cleaning his blade on the troll's scrap of clothing, "is how you kill a troll."

The young knights watched in awe, weapons at the ready. There were enough monsters to go around, and those great reptilian mounts posed a significant threat.

"I'm coming, baby." Laken didn't spout any grand promises to change or prostrate themself before her. *Acta non verba*, was it?

Laken led the charge to Silverstone, Fallon crushing fallen bodies beneath her hooves. Trolls, kobolds, and oversized lizards meant nothing to a seasoned knight, especially of their caliber. And most of these fools only had eyes for the mine, arrogance leaving them open for counterattacks.

They dismounted and backhanded a troll, catching and twisting its arm. It snarled and thrashed, and screamed as Laken used its body to soak up slashes and jabs from its allies. The troll slumped to their feet, where it succumbed to the heel of Laken's boot. Fallon finished it off, just another patch of dirt to the horse.

Charlotte hung back from the fray, comforting one of the young knights. The lad was doubled up and retching his last meal.

Minogue laughed, joining Laken in the fray. "Some of these boys really are green behind the ears!" He wheeled around, slicing open a reptilian's back.

"Yes, but some are holding their own." Laken nodded at two triumphant youngsters and kicked a kobold towards them. "Still, this lot would be long dead if I had a proper team."

"Alas," he said, dancing around several hapless kobolds. "I think the way is clear enough, no?"

"Don't get too excited." Laken stared grimly at the trolls hammering away at the entrance of Silverstone. It was far from luxurious, and easily forgotten compared to those securely in the Queen's land, which worked in their favor.

Essentially a gaping hole in the mountainside, it had one main entrance and a few smaller ones tucked away. Trolls and kobolds clung and dug at these smaller gaps like flies to honey.

Those worried Laken less than the insects scuttling on the ground; Zelamir and her friends were on the main floor. *Their* Zel. Ann when they were alone, Zellie if they were in a teasing mood. Zelamir to friends and acquaintances, Anniken, when they were stern.

But never truly theirs, and all because they had no self-control...

A scream, far too human to be anything else, shocked them out of their head and back to the present.

"Playtime is over," Minogue growled, leaping to the aid of a fallen knight. His sword nimbly danced through the air, so quick as to be missed if blinking.

Laken jerked back as a great reptilian monster rushed them, aided by the slick ground and pouring rain. It was thick around the middle, short legs heavily clawed and low to the ground. Its snake-like jaws snapped in open air, viscous fluid dribbling from its mouth.

Venom.

They'd only encountered such creatures three times in their life and avoided being bitten each time. Laken wasn't going to break that streak now.

The reptile lunged for another bite, but recoiled when it struck steel. Hissing, it came at Laken again, aiming for their side.

"Get out of my way," they snapped, slicing into the monster's thick hide. The reptile slumped over, jaws feebly snapping. It rolled onto its back, clawing and biting at nothing, until its body finally wound down.

Laken stomped on its head and cleaved it clean in half, exposing pulsating organs of vivid cerulean. Charlotte could salvage the venom sacs, if she so desired. Alchemists paid a handsome fee for such a prize, but Laken wanted nothing to do with crafting.

The trolls at the door glanced back at the advancing knights and inched away, grunting and speaking in that strange tongue of theirs. They looked beaten down, scarred over in several places, limbs caked in dried blood. Laken waved at them to approach, but only one had the balls. The other returned to pounding, albeit half-heartedly.

The sole troll advanced, a gnarled club in his hands. He sized them up, nodding appreciatively at Laken's height and sword.

Trolls understood two things: bulk and the efficiency of blades.

He staggered towards them, lifting that mighty club above his head. Laken bit back a laugh. He was slow, painfully so. Not that they were any better; in terms of speed, Minogue, and even Zelamir, had them beat.

But whereas the troll relied on downward motion, Laken favored a well-timed slash. They caught him in the side, and he collided into their shoulder.

Laken grit their teeth, digging their feet into the mud as they sawed through the troll's gut. Pain radiated down their shoulder, down to the bone. Later, Minogue and Charlotte would confirm they heard the crack, the sound of their arm breaking in two different places. To Laken, it just sounded like clanking armor.

They twisted their blade upwards, carving through the troll's body and spilling his intestines, and cleaving off an arm. The whizzing sounds of arrows followed the dazzling stars in their vision, but they blinked it back and shuffled away, picking themself up off the ground.

Laken's sword arm was still functional, so there was that. They leaned on their sword, biting their lip until it bled, a welcome alternative to the pain raging in their arm. Anniken...they had to help.

"Ser," Charlotte pleaded. "It's over. Minogue has—"

"I need to see that with my own eyes."

The troll at the door swayed on its feet, took one step, and fell flat on its back, a blade buried in its heart.

Behind it, peeking out of the rubble and smeared with blood and soil, was Zelamir's pale face. She fought off two of her teammates and ran into the open, and Laken opened their arms to receive her, ignoring the pain in their arm and the falling sword.

And then they were holding her, spinning her around, and kissing her hard in the rain.

19

Don't Look Now

The storm raged on for several more hours, but everyone was inside by then.

Most of the knights retreated to Ashfort, where the villagers welcomed them with open arms. What they lacked in resources and queenly comfort, they made up with warm food, blankets, and shelter for the horses.

Or so Meike heard.

The injured remained tucked away in Silverstone, tended to by Meike and Laken's young squire. Teddy ditched the group to rub elbows with the knights in town. He claimed there was a banquet planned, in honor of the "epic battle".

Knowing the main dishes were bound to be heavily meat influenced, Meike tried not to get too excited.

They washed their hands with water from their canteen. This wasn't the first time they longed for hand sanitizer, but this was good enough.

On either side of them, young men dozed in and out of consciousness. Meike tried feeding them healing potions, but some wounds required good old needle and thread. One man needed a poultice for a nasty bite on his forearm. He'd mumbled something about poisonous lizards before fainting.

It wasn't worth correcting him at the moment, but it might save his life in the future to know the difference between venom and poison.

"Meike, I think it's time." Anniken sat with her back against the wall, Laken's head resting in her lap. She wiped their brow with a handkerchief.

Laken refused treatment until their men were seen to first. "I've had worse," they'd said, grimacing from some unseen injury.

While Meike patched up the others, Charlotte and Anniken coaxed Laken out of their armor. Meike didn't need to examine the knight to know it was bad.

And they looked worse up close.

Stripped of their armor and most of their underclothes, Laken looked smaller, but no less imposing. A nasty bruise stretched from their collarbone to their hip. There was no doubt their arm was broken, and the same could be said for their shoulder as well.

Meike tenderly prodded the darkened flesh around Laken's neck and felt their breath hitch.

"Careful," Anniken snapped. "She's in a lot of pain."

"It's not that bad…" Laken's eyelids flickered, briefly revealing pale eyes. "How are the boys?"

"They're fine. I'm more worried about you right now. Charlotte?"

She was quick to join Meike's side, a small stick in her hands. "Ser, we needed to set your arm hours ago."

Laken's eyes fluttered closed, and they were silent for so long Meike thought they were unconscious. "Get on with it."

Anniken had the honor of holding Laken in place, while Charlotte placed the stick in their mouth. But Meike couldn't do the next step, the biggest, without her.

They'd never set a broken bone before, and never wanted to again.

"You've never done this before, have you?" Charlotte asked.

"No…" They felt sick to their stomach. Laken's arm was massive and almost too perfect to handle.

"Here, hold their shoulder. Let me take the lead."

"…How old are you again?"

"Old enough," she snapped. "Hurry, we've wasted enough time already!"

Meike closed their eyes to avoid the horrific aftermath, but couldn't shut their ears. The first _crack_ made them jump. Laken groaned beneath the gag and tried to jerk away from the finale.

"Ser. This is for your own good." Charlotte successfully wrangled the knight and snapped their arm back in place. "Zelamir, administer the first potion."

Sweat ran down Laken's face as they tentatively sipped the healing liquid. The effects were almost immediate—and borderline disastrous.

It started with a series of tiny pops, like bubbling soda escaping from a can. Laken jerked in place, injured arm outthrust, the skin bubbling and rippling beneath the surface.

"Meike! What's in this potion?" Anniken asked, trying her damnedest to hold Laken still.

"Same as usual...I think it's part of the healing process." They were used to treating scrapes and bruises, not broken bones. Itching was the biggest side effect they knew of until today.

"Aye. Happens all the time," Charlotte said. She was eerily calm. "The quickest fix isn't always the prettiest."

Laken's breath evened out as the potion ran its course, but it was hard to look away.

"Alright Ser," Charlotte said, cheerily as ever. "Time to let those old bones rest!" Together, she and Meike bandaged and splinted Laken's arm. It wasn't pretty, but it was the best they could do. Afterwards, Charlotte waved Meike aside, leaving Laken in Anniken's capable hands.

"I'd hate to move them so soon, but Laken can't stay here." She picked her way around the chamber, straying towards the exit. "The mine isn't an ideal place to host the ill."

"But is the town any better?"

"Ashfort?" She wrinkled her nose. "I wouldn't send my family dog there."

"Then..." She wasn't suggesting Redadore, was she?

"Yeah. The capital. We have better healers—no offense—and the Queen is awfully fond of Laken."

That was all well and good, but how did she expect to pull that off? Laken was in no shape to ride a horse. "But how do we get them there?"

"I have my ways," she said, winking.

Meike soon came to know what that meant, warming up near a small campfire outside of the mine. It was too big of a risk to make inside Silverstone itself, although the knights surely would've appreciated it. Instead, they made do with blankets provided by the villagers.

The villagers also brought what spare food they had, which was largely seafood related: baked fish, dried fish, tiny crawfish, and some very hard potatoes. A far cry from the grand feast Teddy boasted of.

So while it was a disheartening meal for Meike, who had a single potato with their rations, they were glad to be under the night sky, feeling the gentle breeze on their skin.

Even ignoring the damp atmosphere, thickening mud, and fallen trees, it was nice out. Before heading off to the village, a few intact knights stopped to remove the bodies and clear the path to the mine. One even returned to erect the fire and construct a drying rack. Capes and clothes hung from it, fluttering in the light wind.

"Not a single vegetable in sight," Cass remarked, eying her share with disdain. "The men—boys really, bless them—ate what they could, but they aren't accustomed to such paltry meals."

"They'll come around," Charlotte said, eagerly biting into a baked fish. Like the others, it still had its face, lifeless eyes fixated on Char's champing jaws. "You didn't hear Ser Laken complain none."

Laken, despite their fragile state, had enough resolve to admonish the dissenting cries, making the men quake in their beds. "Have you no decency? These kind people gave us shelter, and the very food from their own coffers! They have better home training and grace than you sorry lot!"

"I suppose, but one can't get by on meat alone." Cass sighed and evicted a crawfish from its shell. "But what can I say? I've had worse meals." And then she slurped it up, including the juicy bits stuck in the shell.

Meike shivered and leaned into Vivica's thick fur. She had none of the offered meal, but disappeared after the rain died down to retrieve a rabbit. Vivica was kind enough to eat it away from camp, but a bit of blood stubbornly clung to her upper lip.

"What's your plan?" Meike asked now, eager to change the subject.

"I want to borrow a cart," she said simply. "We can use it to transport Laken back to Redadore. Just need a strong horse or two to pull it."

Meike sat upright, startling Vivica. "We can use my pony! He's really strong."

"Ha, better than Fallon and Madam Felicity. Like their knights, the horses are too prideful to play the role of common draft horses." Seeing the look of confusion on Meike's face, she quickly elaborated. "Fallon is Laken's steed. The other belongs to Minogue. He's the one who chose to stay in town."

"Right...anyway, I already loaned a cart from the village. I don't think they'd mind if we used it."

"Good! It's still too early to move them, but I'll leave the final decision to you."

Meike almost choked on their potato. "You're leaving it up to me?"

"Of course!" She grinned, a scale stuck between her two front teeth. "Doctor's orders, and all that."

They sipped at water to clear their throat, but found it did little to that effect. "Yeah, that's me..."

Doctor! Meike wasn't a doctor! They were a botanist and only went to the hospital as a patient, not a licensed physician.

Luckily, or unluckily, Cass jumped in to smooth things out with Charlotte. "And a damn good one, too. Meike's just a little shy, is all." She gave them the warmest smile, and Meike lowered their eyes, cheeks flushed with embarrassment.

But it felt nice to be acknowledged, even if it was embellished. No, Meike wasn't a doctor in the traditional sense, but they aspired to be a good healer, and a better friend.

"Zel, you should get some rest," Laken said. She awkwardly wiped grease from her chin. Eating was no fun when you were sick. The neck collar didn't help, either.

"I will, once you're taken care of." Anniken pressed a cool cloth against Laken's cheek. She placed another shredded piece of fish into Laken's mouth.

Thank goodness for the privacy shield Charlotte erected, odd as it was. She didn't like being out in the open for all the world to see. Like the lengthy kiss they shared immediately after, for the sake of testing its legitimacy. And of course Laken tried to grab her ass...

Anniken wanted to smack them for being so bold, but Laken looked so sad and broken, like a puppy abandoned on the side of the road. She gave them a pass—for now—choosing to spoil them until they were back at full health. And then they could have a very serious talk about the state and future of their relationship.

But for now...

She set the empty bowl aside and leaned against the cool, gray wall. Just on the other side, vague outlines of Laken's men stirred. Charlotte assured her that the privacy shield was like a one-way window; the people outside couldn't see within.

Were the circumstances different, and they on better terms, then...

"Zel? What are you thinking about?"

She touched her cheek, painfully aware of the heat there. Did Laken notice? "Nothing..." She turned to face the wall. "And you can call me Anniken when it's just the two of us. Zelamir is only an alias."

"I know, but it seemed important to you." Laken shifted and groaned.

Anniken glanced over her shoulder, willing her feet to stay rooted to the ground. "Do you need some help?"

"No, no. It'll pass."

She could only hope Laken didn't have internal bleeding, but weren't there usually signs? Laken wasn't coughing up blood, at least.

"So, um..."

"Yes?"

Anniken coughed and fiddled with her sleeve. "You mentioned that you've had worse injuries."

Laken awkwardly chuckled, whether from Anniken's choice of topic or the pain, it was hard to say. "Is that really what you want to talk about? Old battle wounds?"

"You don't have to. I'm just..." With a sigh, she sank to the floor, hugging her knees to her chest.

"I'm sorry, Annie."

Anniken licked her lips, tongue dry as paper. "I...thank you."

Laken patted the spot beside them. "Can you get closer? I'm trying not to strain my voice."

Of course. Anniken slid on over and was content to feel Laken's arm around her.

"That's better..." Laken nuzzled their cheek against hers. "Did I tell you how much I missed this?" they asked, voice hardly more than a whisper.

Anniken's heart sped up. It was different with the barrier up. No one would know if they...fooled around a little.

"I missed you, too." She kissed their cheek, lingering in place. Did she want to take it further, or give them enough to leave them wanting more?

"You know, this shield doesn't work on sound. We'll have to be...discreet." Laken's hand inched up her thigh.

Really? Quick as a snake, Anniken jabbed Laken's injured shoulder.

They flinched back, hissing. "Shit, Zel! I was only teasing."

"Do you really think now is the time for that?" she hissed back.

Laken placed a hand over their heart. "I'm just trying to stay positive."

"You can't use your injuries as an excuse," Anniken whispered furiously, aware that sound carried far here.

"I've heard from very reputable sources that certain activities can diminish pain."

"Oh, you are so full of shit."

Laken leaned back, shrugging their good shoulder. "You got me. I'm powerless and taking it out on everyone but myself."

Anniken gently punched them in the shoulder. "Oh, Laken...you don't have to get all maudlin on me, either." She reclaimed her spot, snuggling into their side. "I wasn't going to say anything at first, but I do want to talk—about us—when we're safely back in the capital."

"One of those, eh?" They let out a heavy sigh. "Fine. But Annie..."

"Yes?" she asked, when Laken failed to elaborate.

"Can you stay by my side tonight? I'm so tired..."

Anniken squeezed their hand. "Only if you promise to behave yourself."

"I can do that. And besides," they said, kissing her ear, "I want to be at full strength for you."

Oh, why didn't this damn shield have a mute function?

Too flustered to respond with words, Anniken gave Laken one last kiss for the night.

20

LIKE HUMANS DO

Being accosted by a group of near feral children wasn't Meike's idea of a good time, but it was hard to argue with numbers. And it wasn't socially acceptable to hit children, even if they were armed to the teeth.

Marty, the leader of the ragtag bunch, stepped forward. "Adventurer Meike, we come to you with not only a well stocked cart," he said, gesturing behind him at a heap of blankets and rations, "but a request of our own."

"I told you before that you don't need to give me a title, Marty. Not Adventurer, not Doctor, and definitely not Ser."

The kids around him looked uneasy, but Marty...Marty looked like he wanted to puke. "But I have to call you something! Even Ser Barkenshire gets the privilege."

Meike didn't have the heart to tell him that Pickles was just teasing him. "If you have to call me anything, then Capsule will do."

A sense of relief overtook the kids. Little Terry elbowed his way to the front, wooden dagger clutched in his hand, and his real weapon strapped to his side. "We want to see the knight!" He waved the toy in the air, a tiny fierce knight.

"Do you mean Laken?"

"Yes," Marty said. "We got the cart all tidied up for them. And Butterscotch is all fed and rested for the journey ahead."

"I guess it's alright, then. Just try not to overwhelm them. Laken isn't feeling well."

Marty and the kids gave varied acknowledgments; some nodded solemnly, while others brandished their blades and uttered horrific cries.

"Please tone it down before we reach Silverstone. You're going to give someone a heart attack."

Kids being kids, they turned the volume down as they ran headlong down the road and swarmed in front of the mine.

Meike sighed and petted Butterscotch. "Kids are terrifying."

Cass intercepted the children before they reached Laken and had them lined up in three rows. "What do you little ragamuffins want?"

"The knight! The knight!" Terry nearly lost his toy from all the excessive swinging.

"I don't think they want to see *you*," she said curtly. Seeing Meike, she sighed. "Laken isn't in the mood for visitors at the moment—don't give me that!"

The kids collectively groaned, and a few stomped their feet in defiance.

"Cut it out, all of you," Meike said. "And what's gotten into Laken?"

Cass cleared her throat and waved Meike to the side. "They were hoping for a more dignified homecoming."

"What's wrong with the cart?" Sure, it wasn't very glamorous, and couldn't compare to a wheelchair, but what else were they to do?

"You're welcome to talk them into it. I came out here to get some air."

Meike really didn't want to do this. Laken was bedridden, but could take them out with a punch. And Cass expected them to...what? Convince Laken, the Great and Terrible?

"Fine..."

But only two steps in and they already wanted to admit defeat. Laken sat in a corner, surrounded by three figures: Charlotte, Anniken, and Minogue. The other knights were pretending not to overhear the commotion.

"Ser, you we cannot allow you to ride on horseback," Charlotte said. "It's not safe."

"If not by horse, then how do you expect me to get there?"

"By cart," Minogue said. "We—"

"No."

"*No*, Laken?"

"No," they repeated, staring Minogue down. "I won't humiliate myself or our good Queen by reducing myself to mere luggage."

Meike inched back, stopping short when they bumped into Cass. There was no escape.

The two senior knights went back and forth, exchanging crude words Meike dared not repeat. If Minogue couldn't break through to them, what hope did Meike have?

"*Enough*," Anniken suddenly yelled. "Get out." She whipped around, glaring at the young knights. "All of you."

Meike raised their hands and stepped around Cass. The second scariest person here was Anniken, and she even had Laken wincing.

They almost tripped over Terry on the way out. The poor boy's eyes were wet with tears, his little dagger hanging by his side.

"Sorry, Terry. Maybe you can speak to another knight?" Minogue was the strongest contender, being Laken's equal. Meike took Terry's hand and led him away before more unkind words flew.

21

IN A FUNNY WAY

"**I**'m going to be knighted by the Queen's very own sword," Teddy loudly proclaimed, from the front of the procession.

Ser Minogue rode up beside him. "Silence your tongue, boy! That honor is bestowed upon only the most heroic of the land."

The boy went on and on about his adventure in Ashfort, the mine, and the roads leading to them. And now he had delusions...

Anniken wanted to punch him.

She rode abreast of the cart, occasionally taking Laken's hand. They were lucky to have restful sleep, but Anniken found it hard to relax.

Despite the stillness of the night, and the knights guarding the vicinity, Anniken lay waiting for the slap of troll feet on stone.

"Anniken?"

She blinked and studied Laken's placid expression. They were in a constant state of sleeping and waking, made cozy by the quilt laden cart and their own cloak. And to think they wanted to ride home on Fallon...

After Anniken sent everyone off, she sat down and had a very stern conversation with Laken.

"I don't know what's gotten into you," she'd said, holding them by the chin, "but Laken, you know damn well you aren't fit to ride a horse."

"What makes you so certain? Like I said—"

"You've had worse, yes. But this isn't about necessity or even the rush of adrenaline."

Laken stopped fighting her then. "It's a matter of pride, Annie. The mighty Laken, bested by mere trolls?"

"You're not a god, Laken. You're human, much like me and those children."

"Children don't know that until they mature," they'd said as one last act of defiance. "Even Char sees me as infallible."

She took their hand and kissed it. "You shouldn't underestimate her. She cares about you." Otherwise, she'd be a hopeless optimist like Teddy. "If it makes you feel better, I'll tend to you once we're back in the city."

Laken's mouth twitched. "And cater to my every whim?"

"Don't get ahead of yourself," she'd said, unable to restrain a smile. "Here. I'll give you something to make the trip easier..."

"Anniken?"

She blinked, and found herself out on the road, bathed in sunlight. Meike peered back at her.

"Are you alright?"

"I'm fine, just worried." Anniken urged Vallens forward. "I see the guard up ahead," she called out.

"Slow down," Pickles yelled from the comfort of his saddle-bag. "Don't need further casualties."

He was right, of course, but Anniken had no intention of slowing down. Not when they were so close...

The morning sun touched the red buildings in the distance, a warm welcome after dreary days in the dark.

"Faster, Cass!" Pickles yelled.

"Don't involve me in your games, mutt," she said, laughing.

"Be that way, then." He let out a giddy yelp and landed on the ground with a heavy thump.

Anniken spotted orange fur in the corner of her vision. The dog was fast, but he was no match for a horse.

"No fair," Meike yelled, a small voice in the distance. "We're supposed to be a team!"

Minogue just laughed, a bridge between the eager racers and the steady riders. "Let them have their fun. They've been confined long enough."

Anniken glanced back, at the determined Pickles, the lagging Meike, and even the huffing and puffing Teddy.

They were going to be just fine.

Harvest Side Stories

From Friends of Meike

Benekeid Ink, LLC

22

HOT CIDER WITH MAGGIE

Sunlight bathed the garden in a golden hue, fighting the changing foliage for supremacy. Of the few trees in the neatly fenced-in yard, these were all laden with fruit, ripe for the picking. Apples, pears, and plump dragonberries.

A neighborhood cat of short orange fur watched from the fence as the strange woman stepped into the garden. From a distance, one could mistake her figure for human, but come any closer and you were in for the fright of your life.

Maggie set down one of many boxes for the harvest. She sighed and pressed a hand to the small of her back. Youth hadn't completely fled her, but her body wasn't as reliable as it once was. Such was the necessity for hired help, and dear Meike was out adventuring.

She eyed her garden with a weary smile. Common kitchen herbs, along with crops one could only find in forests or far-off lands. A simple spell would safeguard it from the winter months, but like the fruit, this harvest was to be the last of the year.

"I hope you're safe, wherever you are," she said, willing her words to reach her young protégé.

Maggie picked up a fallen apple, turning it over in her rough, green hands. She spat a thick wad of yellowed saliva onto it, rubbed it clean, and tossed the apple, stem and all, into her trap.

The orange cat hissed and stumbled from its perch, landing with practiced ease on white feet.

Apples ran down faster than beasts, being devoid of the complex proteins that made up flesh and bone, and bacteria minuscule.

And that apple, firm but for the small soft spot on the side, was a fine specimen. She decided on turning the lot into cider for the upcoming festivities, but the rest could be sold or bartered.

Demand for dragonberries, those spicy little grapes, was high this time of year. Maggie plopped one into her mouth, where it almost immediately dissolved on her tongue.

Dragonberry wine would also be fine...

Her mouth tingling from the sharpness of the berry, Maggie painstakingly removed vine after vine of berries from the bush. She had to jump a bit to reach a vine snaking through the boughs of a tree, where the sweetest berries dangled just out of reach.

Maggie sighed and rubbed her back. No, she wasn't getting any younger. But all this, before her fifties? She sighed again.

Tonics. There were tonics for this. She'd _made_ some in her youth, for elderly clients, or some unfortunate youth in their twenties.

She just never thought it would be her in need of these services. Oh, to be young and naïve!

Dismay settled on her shoulders as she eyed an apple caught well outside her reach. As a child and even a young woman, she scaled trees with the ease of a squirrel. These days, she was apt to fall and break her back. No, this was a job for Meike or some feckless youth. But there was no harm in letting it fall.

Let the birds and squirrels have at it.

She took great care with the boxes, wheeling them one by one on a handcart. The end goal was the kitchen, where she would inspect and clean the produce before carting them off to their final destination. The berries took lesser priority, requiring extensive picking and cleaning. Her hands prematurely itched at the idea of combing through vines and stems, and removing dirt and debris.

Maggie scrubbed her hands clean before grabbing a colander to separate the fruit from the basin. Humming a childhood tune to herself, she picked up the first of many apples, checked it over for any blemishes or soft spots and, finding its golden sheen endearing, plucked the stem and set it in the colander.

All in all, only three apples failed to pass the test. These she set aside for personal consumption.

Maggie quartered twenty apples and added them to the heavy pot resting on her stove. She topped this off with three oranges to give the cider its bitter tang, along with a host of spices—cloves, cinnamon, nutmeg, ginger—and left the lot to simmer while she tended to the pears and berries.

The pears were to go straight to market, along with a few apples. But the berries! Oh, the berries!

She sat on a stool as she worked the berries free from vine and stem, filling a bucket as she went along. It was truly dull work, but gave her a sense of nostalgia. As a child, she helped out on her aunt's orchard, picking fruit, including grapes. But unlike the crimson dragonberries, grapes came in bunches and required less finesse. Part of the fun of eating them came from plucking them one by one!

But not dragonberries. Those grew like bigger, heavier fruit, on their own spindly stalks. They required individual plucking, as one couldn't simply run their fingers through and come up with several at a time. Oh, she'd tried when she was younger, leaving thin red scratches on her palms and fingers.

Maggie likened them to plucking hairs from her brow, back when she had smooth skin and worried about the dreaded uni-brow.

The fruit was ready for mashing by the time she was done, and she was glad for the change of pace, but her hand cramped something fierce by the end of it. And not from old age, she was sure of that!

Her favorite part (second only to sampling), was straining the lot through a cheesecloth. Were Meike here, she'd rely on the strainer, but there was something satisfying about squeezing the juices out of a cloth! She dumped the dry remains into a bowl. It would make for a nice applesauce, either for herself or one of the neighborhood children.

She mixed in a bit of honey into the batch, and after two samplings, portioned it out into several glass jars.

"This might be my best one yet," she said to her cat. But then again, she said that about every batch.

Maggie set aside a small jar for her young protégé, another for herself, and left the rest for the festivities.

23

MOIRA'S NERVOUS ENERGY

"You've done well for yourself, child."

"Thank you, Madame Claudette," Moira said with all the grace of an esteemed apprentice. Were it anyone else, she would've balked at being called "child". The Madame and like-minded elderly folk were the exception to the rule.

"T'cha," she said, waving an impatient hand Moira's way. "You're still under my tutelage, but you are no longer that shy little lamb who first came to shop, girl. I've told you since your twentieth year to drop the 'madame' and call me Claude or Detta."

Moira paled at the very idea! The Madame was old enough to be her grandmother, and respect for one's elders had been drilled into her head at an early age. And someone of the Madame's standing deserved so much more.

"With all due respect, Madame, I'm afraid I'll have to decline."

"You young chillun..." She gestured again, a motion for Moira to be quiet. "Are these all you're donating to the celebration?"

She spoke of the collection of potions—mostly utility, but a few fluff pieces—scattered on her workbench. The Madame held a thin vial in one hand, admiring the teal liquid within.

"No ma'am. These are but a sample of what I plan to send off."

Every year, at Madame Claudette's insistence, Moira made a batch of potions for the Queen's court mages and knights. Nothing as grand as some alchemists, but it was a gesture well appreciated and, as of late, rewarded. Ten gold wasn't a lot in the grand scheme of things, but Moira happily took and added the funds to her savings.

That's what Madame Claudette would do, and as always, Moira followed her lead.

With hope, a knight of the order or a court mage would take notice of Moira's generosity, and offer to take her under their wing. She smiled grimly at the idea of moving from one master to another, caught in a perpetual state of apprenticeship. She had a head start on many, including the late bloomer, Meike. In a year's time, she would be able to officially cut the cord and strike out on her own...

"Hello there?"

"Hmm?" Moira came out of her reverie, though wasn't entirely present; one foot stayed in the ethereal land of daydreams, while her other foot braced firmly against the edge of reality.

"Where's your head at, child?" The Madame sighed and shook her head. "I thought you promised me you'd quit with the mind wandering!"

"My apologies, Madame Claudette."

She sighed again, this time following it up with a series of rhythmic clicks. "There ya go again! Madame Claudette this, Madame Claudette, that! Bless your heart, child."

Moira demurely closed her eyes and bowed her head. "I was just thinking about the harvest festival."

"Of course you were!" She winked and roughly nudged Moira's shoulder. "Have you got a date, child? You do, don't you? Thinking about some nice young fella, hm?"

"Madame Claudette," she gasped, face turning pale. It wasn't the first time the Madame brought up Moira's love life (or lack thereof).

"You do, don't you? Tell old Detta who. Anyone I know?"

Color restored itself in Moira's cheeks, reddish undertones bringing out the richness of her brown skin. "Not a fella, no...but nothing is official. We're just...really good friends."

"Just good friends, she says! Don't be shy 'round old Detta, now!"

Moira shook her head, the words sticking to her tongue. She thought her intentions were clear enough, but Meike was a tough nut to crack. Everyone but them could see it... "With all due respect, it's nothing I want to discuss at the moment."

"Still in the discovery stage, I see." She smiled, placing a gentle hand on Moira's arm. "Don't rush it. Guard your heart, but don't wait too long, either. Don't you miss out on a good thing, ya hear?"

Moira heard her loud and clear. "May I leave? I should mail these out before the post office closes."

"Yes, of course! Don't let me hold you back."

As much as she wanted to turn heel and fly, Moira forced herself to take controlled steps out of the Madame's tidy home of cozy couches and cushions. One thing she missed was the earthy smell of patchouli and incense, but her head refused to clear until she was breathing the crisp, cool air outside.

"Oh Effie," she mumbled into her sleeve. Her loyal servant was forbidden from materializing in the Madame's home, after an unfortunate incident with an antique teapot.

The tiny token warmed her wrist where it was tied. Even bound, Effie tried to soothe her spirits!

"You'll be out soon, I promise. Just give me time to see these off..."

Madame Claudette lived a good twenty minutes from the city square. It was faster by horse or cart of course, but Moira had neither at the moment. It would be even shorter with Effie's assistance, a suggestion surely befitting Meike.

Meike...

"I sure hope they're alright," she said, worrying the token in her sleeve. "It's almost harvest time, and I just know Meike will be disappointed if they miss out." Harvest season was the biggest occasion of the year, second only to the winter festivities.

She handed the package to the mail clerk and paid the small postage fee. There were more instantaneous means of transport, but Moira liked the slow and steady work of a pigeon. Less room for error, in her opinion. A colleague of hers once lost an entire parcel of precious gems, because of a simple typographical error.

"Thank you, that will be all." Her eye lingered on handmade cards with cutesy woodland critters. Meike would enjoy those...but Moira had an even better idea. Something that couldn't be so easily packaged and forwarded, an *experience*.

She called forth Effie in a quaint alley, not for the sake of mere transport, but to have the pleasure of company.

"You know, Effie, I do have a newer model at home. A PDA, I mean. And while I don't know Meike's call sign, I still know the model code and number. I could send them a little poke..."

Effie nodded along. "I do believe Meike would enjoy that."

"I'll keep it light! Simple..." She twiddled her thumbs now. How should she go about this? Should she change her call sign to something more...recognizable? She'd hate for Meike to write her off as some unknown harasser...

At home, Moira switched her stiff, formal robes for a light gown. She hadn't been entirely honest with Meike before. That old AC she gave them wasn't the only device in her possession, but it was a primitive old thing she'd gotten in her girlhood. Any respectable alchemist kept an upgraded device at hand, for the sake of easy communication and keeping up with the times.

And this latest model cost her a month's wages.

Moira fished it out of her bedside table, a palm sized device with a smooth bottom made of blue obsidian. Beautiful. Delicate. *Hers*.

She traced a symbol on the screen, the purplish blue of the Mythic Script lingering for but a second. Mana channeled into the device, illuminating the screen beneath her fingertip.

The caricature of a felibog, a curious creature that resembled a cat with the bushy tail of a fox, danced along her screen, chasing its own tail into oblivion. And then with a wink it was gone, the screen settling on several containers, containers that denoted several functions and servers.

One in particular, shaped like a pair of pursed lips, was accompanied by the number twenty-five. Twenty-five unread messages from Wysper, better than any pigeon or even Effie's wondrous leaps. The brunt of these surely came from the local alchemist group; Moira was connected to the main organization at large, but kept it silenced so as not to disturb her work or rest with frivolous or irrelevant complaints and requests.

None of that mattered now, just Meike. Giving them a pleasant surprise, a welcome voice in a dark place. They could talk for hours and hours about plans for this harvest season, of the food and drink, the games...

And maybe, were she bold enough, Moira could even lay it all down. Bear her heart, and chance a kiss under the light of the full moon. Silly fantasies best left in romance novels and daydreams, but she was still young and very capable of dreaming, of loving, of hoping.

Moira opened a private channel for just her and Meike, a simple one to accommodate their unrefined AC. Meike's didn't have extensive access to the Wysper system, but direct communication was still possible, if slow.

Yet when it came to the message itself, Moira's mind went blank.

She swallowed the lump forming in her throat, and finding it dry, fixed herself a glass of water.

You couldn't go wrong with a simple hello, but that left the pressure on Meike to prompt discussion, did it not? No, she should at the very least introduce herself...

Hello, Meike! It's me, Moira. You're probably wondering how I

She frowned, clicked her teeth, and erased the message.

Hey Meike! It's me, Moira!

No, too eager...

Moi

Hey Meike! It's me, Moira. Just reaching out to see how you're doing, and what your plans are for the holiday.

Satisfied with this version, she sent it off into the aether.

24

MIGHTY JABBERJACQUE

The ship pitched viciously from side to side, washing salt water over the straining sailors. Human, ogre, and beastfolk alike thrashed and strained to remain on board, for to be washed out to sea meant death.

Caught among them was a cat with dark blue fur, almost black from frequent drenching.

It hissed through gritted teeth, renewing its efforts to climb the mast. Wind. That old fool of a fisher was going to get them all killed.

Captain Rogeir yelled something unintelligible, but Patches liked to think ae told it to loose the sails. Loose the sails and be free of this wretched monster.

Patches flattened its ears against its head and tensed every muscle in its body. It waited for the ship to give another lurch before springing into the air, propelled further by the rocking of the boat.

Beneath its grasping paws, Patches caught a glimpse of the pink back of the legendary whale, Jabberjacque.

It was such a shame to kill such a creature, but the whale wasn't innocent. How many ships had it destroyed in its twenty years reign? How many sailors were drowned or marooned on unmarked islands?

Among the roar of the storm and screams, one voice could be heard above all. That damn fisher, Everick.

"Don't back down now, lads," he called. "We've almost got the bastard!" He manned the harpoon, both arms wrapped around the device, anchoring it to the ship.

Sir Everick, a legend in his own right. He'd slain several mythical monsters from the deep sea, from giant squids to man-eating tortoises. The whale was his latest obsession, and he vowed to bring its corpse to the great harvest celebration in Redadore.

Patches closed its eyes, trusting the weight of the rope in its paws. This wasn't the worse day of its life, but it came close enough. Thick canvas struck its cheek with enough force to send it toppling head over heels, but it held firm.

And suddenly, the tides were turned in their favor. The sharp wind from the storm pummeled the sails, forcing a tug of war between the whale and ship.

The stench of fresh blood and blubber assaulted Patches' sensitive nose. Its tail bristled and swished behind it as the cat hopped from mast to mast, letting loose the sails and furthering the tugging effect.

The trophy fisher hooted and howled as the whale struggled in vain, the gash in its side becoming more and more prominent, loosing its lifeblood into the roiling water.

"Come on, lads! Put your backs into it!"

Sir Everick's fishers leaned over the ship and stabbed at the snared whale with spears. If it didn't bleed out from its wounds, it would die from shock and trauma.

Patches shivered from its perch. It gave its body a brisk shake, but the water stubbornly clung to its fur. A proper bath would have to do, but that wouldn't be for another week or so.

Captain Rogeir abandoned aer post to catch an overenthusiastic salamander by the arm. "Enough! All of you! You're tearing the damn creature to shreds."

The salamander lowered his head. "But, Captain…"

"No buts!" Ae tore the spear from his hands and flung it onto the deck. "Everick, you know as well as I do that the meat won't last if the beast is allowed to rot at sea."

"Aye, that be true." He smiled, showing off a mouth of gold teeth. "But we can't blame the crew for being excited, can we? It's not everyday you strike down the mighty beast of the sea."

"Don't forget the sharks and other scavengers. We wouldn't want it to arrive half eaten, either."

"Good points, aye, good points all around!" To the fishers, he called out, "Let's get it bagged and ready to tow back to land!"

Patches watched as the stab happy crew exchanged their spears for a net that glimmered like chain mail and spread it out like a massive blanket.

Jabberjacque feebly thrashed in defiance, an act that only tightened its bonds, like a rabbit caught in a snare.

"Poor bastard," the Captain bitterly muttered to aerself.

"Weep not, my kindhearted Captain," Sir Everick said, baring his golden teeth in a fearsome grin. "He would kill you in a heartbeat, without an ounce of remorse."

"Of that I'm sure. I'm just...not fond of the slaughter."

Patches, sensing the mounting tension between its Captain and the Sir fisher, scrambled down beside aer. It waved to catch aer attention, before signing, *Captain, I believe the storm is dying down. Should we continue at our current speed?*

Ae waved an impatient hand at Sir Everick, who rudely stepped between them. *Carry on as is. I don't want our catch spoiling mid-sail*, they signed back.

"What did it say?" Sir Everick's eyes shifted from side to side. "I don't speak gestures."

"Patches just wanted a bit of direction. We are to continue at top speed to our destination." The Captain made a point of standing in Patches' line of view. "Is there anything else I can help you with?"

Sir Everick once again put his back to Patches, but the widening of the Captain's eyes said enough.

Ae was well-respected among this side of the country and even abroad, but Captain Rogeir occasionally had to put men like Everick in their place.

The Captain's eyes settled back to aer usual stern gaze. Ae briefly vanished from its sight, and Everick turned with a sneer.

"—learn to relax," was all Patches caught before the man strode off.

"What a pain, that man..." Ae sighed, weariness creeping into aer eyes. "I'll be glad to be done with him and his lot."

Patches cupped a paw over one ear and motioned for aer to sign. *It's too loud.*

The Captain chuckled and bowed aer head. *My apologies. If it's hard for me, it must be even harder on you.*

It shrugged and clapped its hands. *I casted a dampening spell on myself when that one boarded our ship.*

Ae cupped a hand over aer mouth. *He's a stain on the St. Espeth.* Ae slapped Patches on the shoulder. *Come, let's see that these sea dogs get the whale hauled on deck.*

Patches rubbed its back and made a pained expression. It stumbled forward, taking exaggerated steps.

Oh hush! You aren't an old cat yet! I'll treat you to some cherry wine, how does that sound?

Its eyes widened in delight. *Throw in an anchovy pastry and I'm in.*

Patches dropped the act and sprinted to the massive haul being dragged on board. A whale of this size could feed a whole town, or even half of Laeford.

It gave the whale a curious sniff, mouth watering. And then froze, as a heavy hand landed on its back.

"Don't gobble up the fish without us," the husky dogman said. He grabbed Patches by the tuft of fur on its back, not quite scruffing it, but close enough. He hauled Patches back, sending it skidding along the soaked deck.

Patches' tail swished low to the ground, a growl rising in its throat. Clearly wasn't one of St. Espeth's crew, otherwise he'd be sharply reprimanded by the Captain.

For now, the dog would have to be tolerated.

It thought of the citizens and families of its mates, waiting at home for them. Those jolly faces and gurgling bellies would make this ordeal worth the effort.

25

JUST 5 MORE MINUTES...

It was a cool autumn night, the first of many. The hearth was empty, allowing a chill to settle in the room. It necessitated the need for a warm blanket, which was currently wrapped around the slumbering figure on the small bed.

The soft tinkle of a bell overrode the wind outside, rousing the girl.

"Five more minutes, Ser...that's all I ask."

Charlotte hadn't had a restful night of sleep since they set out to the mine. First, it was the trolls, now it was the injured Laken to tend to.

She sighed as she rolled out of bed. A knight didn't complain about the aches in their feet or arms, but Charlotte was no knight.

Yet.

The bell twinkled again, but Charlotte could hardly complain; it was her idea to give them the damn thing. Just like it was her idea to return to the manor, rather than the castle.

The Queen was more than happy to have them, but Charlotte insisted her dear knight needed an extended leave. One that wasn't in the castle proper, or highly trafficked by servants and curious onlookers, or even the Queen herself.

Charlotte may be just a squire from one of the lesser houses, but she carried herself well, and could be quite convincing.

"The fresh air will do Ser Laken well," she'd said. "She'll have the servants, myself, and her beloved to see to her needs and wants."

Queen Illora had smiled grimly at those words, but didn't push the issue further. She was kind enough to send them off with provisions from her own larder—all matters of meat, cheeses, cakes, and a cask of wine.

Charlotte groaned as she wrapped a robe around her bed clothes and stumbled across the dark room. Life at the manor came with its pros and cons. She had no privacy in the castle, but the fireplace was always stoked. Here, she had her own room, but lacked the energy to build a fire.

For herself, anyway.

"Coming, ser," she called out, just as the dreaded ringing started up again.

The halls were chillier. Usually Laken helped tend to the heating, but that responsibility currently fell on Charlotte. The servants weren't too keen on her, for whatever reason. Old Finch wouldn't crawl out of bed this early, and the servant girls were hired more for their beauty than their worth.

Charlotte stifled a yawn as she stumbled into Laken's bedroom. "How can I be of service, ser?"

In the massive bed (Charlotte's was scarcely bigger than her cot at the castle) laid two figures—the bandaged Laken and her beloved. Laken smiled at Charlotte over Zelamir's bare shoulder.

"Char, would you be a dear and revive the fire? It seems to have gone out."

"And so it has..." The room was far from cold, but the dying embers cloaked the room in darkness. "Right away, ser..."

Laken mumbled something to the woman in her arms, sweet words that drew a light blush to Charlotte's cheeks. The two lovers had recently coupled; it showed in the sweat glistening on their bodies, Zelamir's unsteady breath, and the rumpled bedding.

Charlotte pretended not to hear as Zelamir giggled. She tuned them out, favoring the soft crackle of the embers. The room came alive as she fed the flames wood split by Laken's own axe. It would be awhile before they could swing like that again.

That herbalist, Meike, did a fine job of patching her up, but potions could only do so much.

The extent of Laken's wounds left her bedridden for days, in and out of fever. Charlotte and Zelamir tended to her in equal parts, with the occasional visit from a court doctor.

She was set to recover in a few days, though she'd need to do some physical therapy to the doctor's satisfaction.

Charlotte stepped back from the steadily crackling fireplace. It would tide them over until late morning, when that old man crept out of bed to prepare breakfast.

"Is there anything else I can do for you, ser?"

"Not now, Char, thank you." Laken sighed and laid back, hugging Zelamir close.

Charlotte gave a low bow and crept out of the room, silently closing the door behind her. She'd stayed in the room long enough to warm her body, but now the chill was setting in.

She had a mind to make her own fire. There was plenty of wood at hand, and after getting Laken settled, it was a breeze. But she was just so tired...

It must be nice to have a warm body to cuddle up with on these cold autumn nights...maybe she should get a dog. A big bear of a dog, like the one she was raised with. He shed an awful lot, and smelled persistently of wet fur and whatever he rolled in, but he had a good heart.

Charlotte considered herself too young for other forms of companionship, but the truth was she saw little appeal in it. Laken teased her, saying she'd change her mind in a few years, once she "peaked". Whatever that meant...

Yawning, she eyed the cold hearth of her bedroom, and decided she'd like that fire, after all.

She lined the fireplace with two split logs and a few sticks, and crouched low to the ground, hands clasped. Fire danced along her fingertips and onto the dry kindling. Within seconds there was an uneven crackling as the flames spread from stick to wood.

The problem with magical flame was that it didn't last. It was a bandage over a superficial wound, whereas the flame she sparked for Laken was true.

Charlotte freely yawned on her way back to bed. She had at least two hours before the fire died down, but those precious few hours would cloak her quarters with warmth. Best of all, Laken would have no reason to rouse her.

And if she did, Charlotte could always feign ignorance. Let her darling *Zelamir* put in the work.

Afterword

Hello, and thanks again for joining me on this journey through Glasend! I had a lot of fun writing this book, though I'm still finding my footing. Not all books will focus on a singular dungeon or area, but this was a special case.

I originally wrapped up season three after Laken arrived at the mine, but wanted to add a bit of closure. You got a touch of that in Charlotte's Harvest story, but I wanted to do something extra for the book release. Like the special formatting for the text messages.

And speaking of texting...

While it is something I want to do more of in the future. I promise not to overdo it, though. Too much kinda kills the vibe, ya know? But I had a lot of fun staging it, which required some chopping and editing to make it easier to read. Honestly, it was nice that the story allowed use for the feature.

Especially considering the lack of technology...

But that's what makes magitech so much fun! And the odd little phones are just a taste of what Glasend has to offer. There's a major innovation Moira is working on, in conjunction with her guild and others. I can't say more than that without spoiling it, but I can only hope y'all enjoy it!

And yes, the title of this book is a Junji Ito reference. It's been meme'd so much that people unfamiliar with the source material can quote it. But if that means nothing to you, and you are a fan of horror, I highly recommend reading *The Enigma of Amigara Fault*. It's more eerie than outright scary, in my opinion. *Tomie* was my introduction to Ito, and that's a series I wouldn't hand to a newcomer, same with *Uzumaki*. But I'll save the recs for my blog.

If you want to read new chapters of Last Train Home, you can do so directly on my blog, by subscribing to the Portal Enthusiasts tier. As a subscriber, you'll also receive short stories involving Meike or side characters, your name in acknowledgments of future books, and early access to ebooks before the general public.

About The Author

Eggler is a queer, trans, and autistic author of queer fiction with sapphic leads and the occasional romance. Ey write primarily fantasy (low, portal, and urban) and sci-fi, but have a deep love for the horror genre. Elements of horror can be found throughout eir work, but ey have yet to pen anything strictly in that genre.

When not writing, ey like to play indie adventure games, visual novels, and pine over sapphic vampires. Occasionally hike, when the weather and allergies allow. Ey live in northeast Ohio with eir partner and two cats.

You can learn more about em on eir blog at www.sienn aeggler.com/, where you can subscribe to eir newsletter for updates and news about future books.

www.ingramcontent.com/pod-product-compliance
Lightning Source LLC
Chambersburg PA
CBHW021949120726
47992CB00001B/215